A Deadly Distance

A Deadly Distance

Heather Down

A SANDCASTLE BOOK
A MEMBER OF THE DUNDURN GROUP
TORONTO

Editor: Michael Carroll
Designer: Jennifer Scott
Printer: Marquis Book Printing

Library and Archives Canada Cataloguing in Publication

Down, Heather, 1966-
    A deadly distance /Heather Down.

ISBN 978-1-55002-637-5

    1. Beothuk Indians--Juvenile fiction. I. Title.

PS8607.O95D42 2006   jC813'.6   C2006-904263-2

1   2   3   4   5   11   10   09   08   07

Conseil des Arts du Canada   Canada Council for the Arts   Canadä   ONTARIO ARTS COUNCIL
CONSEIL DES ARTS DE L'ONTARIO

We acknowledge the support of the **Canada Council for the Arts** and the **Ontario Arts Council** for our publishing program. We also acknowledge the financial support of the **Government of Canada** through the **Book Publishing Industry Development Program** and **The Association for the Export of Canadian Books**, and the **Government of Ontario** through the **Ontario Book Publishers Tax Credit** program and the **Ontario Media Development Corporation**.

Care has been taken to trace the ownership of copyright material used in this book. The author and the publisher welcome any information enabling them to rectify any references or credits in subsequent editions.

J. Kirk Howard, President

Printed and bound in Canada
www.dundurn.com

Dundurn Press
3 Church Street, Suite 500
Toronto, Ontario, Canada
M5E 1M2

Gazelle Book Services Limited
White Cross Mills
High Town, Lancaster, England
LA1 4XS

Dundurn Press
2250 Military Road
Tonawanda, NY U.S.A.
14150

*To the memory of my great-grandparents,
Jacob and Phoebe Manuel, who carved a life
in a land of rock and sea*

ACKNOWLEDGEMENTS

Many thanks go to the helpful staff of the Provincial Archives of Newfoundland and Labrador in St. John's and the personable staff at the Mary March Regional Museum in Grand Falls. Thank you, Ben Cox, for answering most of my questions about where and when people lived. Thanks also to my uncle, Harold Manuel, for taking me by boat to Exploits Island — twice.

Acknowledgements

Chapter 1

Startled, Mishbee gasped, frozen with horror. She was staring down the barrel of a musket and was familiar with the sound those weapons made. The young Beothuk girl knew muskets meant death. In an instant she vividly replayed the images of the recent burial of a cousin: red ochre smeared over his body, his most prized possessions gathered for the ceremony. She remembered, as if only moments ago, sneaking off several days after his burial to the cave where he was laid to rest. Her cousin, she understood, would sleep until his spirit travelled to the New Land. Now she wondered if he had arrived at that place yet and if she would join him there all too soon. The cousin had been shot by a settler, and here Mishbee stood facing a settler's gun.

How could she have been so careless? This would never have happened under normal circumstances. It was impossible for a settler to be quiet enough to sneak up on her people. Last spring her father had told her how he and several others were only a stone's throw from a large group of them. Her people were so quiet and still compared to the loud and clumsy settlers that they hadn't been detected. Mishbee's father and the others had remained there until the sun had set in the sky and the settlers had gone home.

But Mishbee was in a different world today. She was gathering blueberries and had been daydreaming. This coming winter her sister, Oobata, would marry Dematith. Her thoughts had drifted to the upcoming ceremony. Mishbee loved winters. Although the weather was cold, furs kept her warm and there were always celebrations, dances, stories, and lots of singing. This winter would be extra special with a wedding. The feast would be an entire day and night filled with wonderful festivity.

Dematith had carved a complex geometric design on whalebone to create an intricate pendant for his future sister-in-law. He had moulded it with much care and patience, and it was Mishbee's most valued treasure. She had been thinking, breathing, and dreaming about the coming winter for months. Unfortunately for Mishbee, it appeared now that these dreams would be all she would ever have to call her own.

Although it felt like hours, all these thoughts raced through Mishbee's head in a matter of a few seconds. A boy, almost a man, sighed behind the musket and said, "I should have stayed in England."

If Mishbee could have understand what he had said, she would have wholeheartedly agreed with him.

"I was never good at shooting anything," he spoke softly to himself.

The boy was perhaps a little older than Mishbee. She was determined not to flinch as she stared into the eyes of her killer. The boy's hair was light with a slight reddish hue. The stranger had deep blue eyes that resembled the ocean, and his cheeks were peppered with brown spots.

He didn't look like her people, yet there was something pleasant about his appearance.

"I've never seen anyone like you," the boy whispered. "Don't tell my trout-fishing partner Allen that I didn't shoot you. He's on the far hill, past the pond." The young man pointed in the direction of the pond behind him. "P-o-n-d," he repeated, stretching out each sound of the short word. The boy shook his head. "Allen and I got separated somehow. He'd shoot you in a second, you know. His father was killed by one of your people during a raid, and he's never gotten over it. It was a terrible tragedy."

The young man continued to stare at Mishbee's jet-black hair, which was decorated with a simple feather nestling in her single braid. Mishbee wondered what he saw. She knew she was taller than most of the other girls of her tribe, and she was proud of the red ochre that glistened on her skin in the sunlight like the sparkles in the nearby pond.

The strange boy sighed once more and shifted his weight to one hip. Mishbee wondered when her death would finally come. Even though she mustered all the control deep within her soul, her left leg began to tremble. At first it was just an irritating twitch, but the more she tried to stop it, the more her leg shook.

The boy seemed to notice her shaking and suddenly snapped out of his trance. "What am I doing? I'm so sorry. Please don't worry. I have no intention of hurting you. I'm not much of a hunter. The other settlers tell terrible stories and say your people kill us and raid our settlements, that you're savage and unspeakably cruel. But looking at you, I can't believe any of that. You're just gathering food from the woods like anyone else would. Don't be afraid. You can go. Please, go ..." He cocked his head and motioned sideways with the gun.

Although Mishbee had heard the sound of muskets, she had never actually seen one fired. Watching the stranger's gestures, she thought this sideways movement was how the weapon was ignited. When the boy motioned to the side, she gasped and braced herself for certain death. When she didn't hear the thunderous noise, her fear became immeasurable and her trembling intensified.

"Go on, please," the boy begged, repeating the gesture.

This was too much for Mishbee. Feeling that she was once more preparing for death, she closed her eyes.

Then the boy did an amazing thing. Slowly, he placed his musket on the ground in front of him, carefully took three steps backward, and sat on a nearby rock, where he made an effort to stay still. "Surely distance can't hurt," he said, raising his hands high in the air. "Please, *please*, go."

Bewildered by yet another wave of his hand, Mishbee wondered if this monster was giving her life back to her. The elders had always told her that the first white men that had come over the Great Lake were from the Good Spirit and that those who had come next were sent by the Bad Spirit. Maybe this boy was from the Good Spirit. Was that possible?

Gripped with uncertainty and fright, she took one small step backward. The boy didn't move. She took another step, and he remained as immobile as a settler was capable of, watching her intently. In one sweeping motion, she turned, half expecting to hear the boom of the musket and to inhale her final breath. As she fled, a branch caught the leather string that held her precious pendant around her neck, causing it to break and fall into the brush. Heartbroken by the loss of her pendant, yet fearful for her very existence, Mishbee kept running.

Chapter 2

Disappointed, embarrassed, relieved, and saddened at the same time, Mishbee returned to her people's summer gathering. Besides losing her prized pendant, she had also dropped her blueberries in the confusion and wasn't sure how she was going to explain her empty-handed state to her family and friends.

Luckily for Mishbee, most of her people were out at the small island cliffs hunting great auks. Many others were fishing. A small number were still harvesting berries as Mishbee was supposed to be doing. Her mother and Oobata were sitting outside the wigwam, tending the fire and making soup. Mishbee noted how the mixed grease and oxidized rock used to create the sacred and practical red ochre glistened on their skin. Besides being used in celebrations and ceremonies, the lotion served as excellent protection against the sun and was a remarkable insect repellent.

Mishbee's mother greeted her daughter quizzically, brushing away several strands of her own long dark hair that had escaped her braid and fallen across her face. Loving but also stern, Mishbee's mother knew how hard it was to survive in this land. Winters were difficult and food wasn't always plentiful. There was no room for carelessness or mistakes, and children had to be taught that if they were to survive. Mishbee's mother wouldn't be pleased with what had happened today.

"You're back already, Mishbee," her mother said.

"Yes, I …" she answered cautiously, feeling as if her mother could see right through her. Worried that she would have to explain herself, Mishbee tried to divert her mother's attention. "What's in the soup today, Mother?"

"Murre and kittiwake," her mother said, stirring the birds she was cooking by continually putting hot rocks from the fire into the birchbark pot.

Mishbee's mother looked at her intently. Did she notice the missing berries? Would Mishbee have to explain herself, after all? Just as her mother's lips parted to say something, several men, including Dematith, strode into the temporary camp carrying seabirds they had hunted at the cliffs. The arrival of the food allowed Mishbee to dodge her mother's questioning eyes.

"How are you, Little Bird?" Dematith asked, smiling.

Mishbee liked his pet names for her and his easy manner. She was pleased that Oobata would soon be his wife. Mishbee breathed deeply and began to relax a little. "Look at all those birds, Dematith! You had a good hunt."

Dematith put down the auks and looked squarely at Mishbee. "Yes, Little Bird, we had an excellent hunt. I'm tired and hungry now. You wouldn't know what it's like to work so hard."

"I worked all day long, too!" Mishbee said indignantly, speaking with mock authority as if reprimanding him harshly. She enjoyed bantering with Dematith.

Her relief turned to panic, though, when her future brother-in-law peered at her strangely. "Where's your pendant, Little Bird? Don't you like it anymore?"

Mishbee gasped, and her head began to spin. She couldn't possibly explain the missing pendant to Dematith. She had to think fast. "I … I put it in our wigwam."

Mounting confusion filled her. She didn't know what to do. If she went back to find the pendant, she could easily meet an uncertain fate, but how could she explain her carelessness to her family? Her thoughts tumbled uncontrollably. Then she knew what she had to do. With most of her people focused on the men returning from the hunt, Mishbee stealthily retraced her steps back into the woods. When she approached the blueberry patch, she silently floated from tree to tree like a phantom. Her movements went unnoticed except by the most sensitive animals.

Then, to her surprise, Mishbee caught sight of her birchbark basket. It sat upright, half filled with berries on the rock where the stranger had sat. She had only just covered the bottom of the basket before she had made her abrupt departure. Beside the basket, Mishbee was delighted to see her pendant repaired and whole again. Maybe this boy was sent by the Good Spirit, after all.

Mishbee sat absolutely still for over an hour, watching, waiting for signs of the stranger who had earlier caught her unaware. When she was sure no one was lurking, ready to spring a trap, she slunk cautiously to the rock. She picked up her pendant and hung it proudly around her neck, then gathered up her berry basket and sneaked back to her hiding place to wait for the stranger to return. He had spared her life and put berries in her basket. Convinced that the kind gesture wasn't a trap, she wanted to reciprocate his goodwill.

A long time passed before Mishbee heard rustling in the trees. She had almost begun to believe the boy wouldn't return and was nearly ready to head home when the stranger noisily appeared from the brush. Wearily, he walked over to where the berries and pendant had been placed, put his musket on the ground, and slowly lowered himself onto the damp rock.

Unnoticed, Mishbee slid into the open area in plain sight. The boy was still looking in the other direction, and she was able to get close enough to touch him on the shoulder. Then she spoke a greeting.

Startled to hear a voice, the boy jumped back and whirled around with his fists clenched tightly in front of him. "Who's there?" he cried. When he saw who it was, he took a deep breath, relaxed his hands, and smiled. "You scared me. I guess we're even now. Where did you come from?" He stared at Mishbee for a moment, then said, "Hmm, where are my manners? My name's John Harper." He tipped his hat forward in a polite gesture.

Mishbee held up her pendant and nodded, hoping to thank this stranger for rescuing her dearest possession. Tentatively, she picked up a small green branch from the ground and motioned for the stranger to take it from her.

John was surprised by this dark-haired girl's gesture and wondered what it meant. Apprehensive about what might happen if he did *not* take the branch, he pulled the unusual gift close and nodded to show appreciation.

She seemed delighted with his action, and her eyes danced with what John believed was excitement. He pointed at the pendant. "Carve," he said, motioning with his hands as if he were deeply engaged in creating a carving himself. "I carve, too. Except I carve out of wood. Most say I'm very good with wood."

The girl delicately fingered her pendant. John could tell that the carving somehow held great significance for her. He knew what it meant to value a possession. Sticking his hand in his pocket, he traced the outline of the circumference of his father's gold watch. He remembered with pride when his father said to him just before he left England, "See this watch, son? It was my father's once. But now you're almost a man. It's time you have this." Then he placed the timepiece in John's shaky hands. John recalled being a small boy watching his father faithfully wind the heirloom and care for it with great pride. Maybe this girl's pendant was equal in value and sentiment to his treasured gift from his father.

John looked up at Mishbee. "I can tell you love that pendant probably the same way I love my watch."

They stood in silence for a moment. Then the girl abruptly turned and began topping off her berry basket as if John were invisible.

He didn't know what to do with himself. Should he leave or should he stay? He watched as the girl ignored him and picked her berries. "Could you grace me with your name?" he asked, trying to divert her attention from the berries.

Mishbee kept picking.

"Your name?" he repeated, this time louder.

The girl didn't even bother to look in his direction.

Realizing he wasn't getting very far with his attempts to communicate, John walked up to the girl and gently tapped her shoulder with his forefinger. She glanced up at him questioningly. "I'm John," he said, indicating himself. "John." Then he pointed at her.

She smiled and nodded. "Mishbee."

"Mishbee," he repeated triumphantly.

She kept working at her task. John still felt strangely out of place, so he busied himself by picking a small bouquet of everlasting daisies in a small nearby clearing. When he was finished, he brought the flowers to Mishbee and held them out. "These are for you. Some people call them dead man's flowers and others call them everlasting daisies. I'm not sure why they have two names. I guess two different people can look at the same thing and have very different ideas."

Mishbee studied him quizzically, obviously not having a clue what he was doing or saying. Suddenly sensing his naivety, John felt embarrassed and silly. He pulled the flowers back to his side. "I guess you don't have a vase or a front parlour to display these in, so I'll take them home."

The girl glanced at her basket, then turned to leave. John could see that the basket was full. "Where are you going?" he asked.

Mishbee didn't answer. Instead, she left as quickly and quietly as she had come, disappearing into the brush. John knew better than to try to follow her. Danger might lie ahead. There was nothing left for him to do except head back to find Allen.

CHAPTER 3

"Where have you been?" Mishbee's mother scolded, obviously not impressed by her daughter's disappearance. Mishbee was no stranger to the woods, but her absence had been longer than usual.

"I had to finish picking the blueberries."

"The sun will soon set, Mishbee, and there's much work to do here. This isn't the time to wander off. You're needed. Please don't disappoint me with your actions again."

Mishbee hung her head in shame. "I'm sorry, Mother." She was more repentant than her mother knew. The events of the day had caused her greater grief than she cared to think about.

Still, her mother was right. After a hunt, there was always a lot to do. First, Mishbee placed her berries on a flat rock where the other berries were already laid to dry for tomorrow's sun. The air surrounding the rock was filled with a sweet berry aroma. Besides blueberries, the women and children picked partridgeberries, marsh berries, raspberries, and currants at various times in the summer. Their only way of preserving this precious fruit was to dry it in the sunlight or store it in oil. While Mishbee worked diligently, Dematith walked by.

"How are you, Little Bird?" he asked, smiling. "I see you found your pendant." He seemed pleased at the sight of the shiny carving once again hanging around Mishbee's neck.

"Yes" was all Mishbee said, keeping her head down to avoid his eyes.

"Why are you so sullen, Little Bird?" Dematith asked, his tone changing from cheeriness to genuine concern.

As much as Mishbee usually enjoyed talking playfully with Dematith, she wanted this conversation to end. She had a secret and didn't want to reveal it. "I'm not sad, Dematith. I'm just grateful to be wearing your pendant again. I didn't mean to disappoint you earlier."

Dematith sat and wrapped an arm around Mishbee's shoulders. "Don't sound so dejected, Little Bird!"

Mishbee was happy to have Dematith for a friend, since she had never had a brother, only her one sister, Oobata.

"I was only teasing you earlier," he told her. "I know you appreciate my work."

There was never any question in Mishbee's mind that Dematith's carving was treasured. It had almost cost her life, but she couldn't tell him that. "Yes, of course Dematith," she said in her most convincing voice.

Dematith seemed satisfied with Mishbee's response and walked away to help some of the others.

Mishbee went to attend to the fire with Oobata. With such a good hunt of great auks, it would be necessary to keep the birchbark pots filled with birds. Birchbark, or *paushee*, as her people called it was so important. The versatile material was used to make the skins of containers, summer wigwams, and canoes.

"Where were you today?" Oobata asked, not wasting any time with her questions. She was always a keen observer and very direct.

It seemed that Mishbee couldn't escape questions today. "Picking berries," she told her sister.

Oobata glanced around carefully. A couple of women were working at the next fire. She leaned closer to Mishbee and whispered, "Mishbee, Mother isn't around. I know you better than anyone else and can see you're not telling me everything. What secret are you keeping?"

"What makes you think I've got a secret?"

"I just know it. You can't fool me."

Not only was Oobata her older sister, she was Mishbee's closest friend. She had been there from the day Mishbee was born and was like a second mother to her. Oobata could sense Mishbee's joy and dismay before anyone else. Mishbee peered into the dark, solemn eyes of her older sister. Oobata had Mishbee's complexion but was taller than Mishbee and very wise.

"Mishbee," Oobata said, "you're skilled in the woods. It would never take that long for you to fill that tiny basket with berries. And why didn't you have your pendant when you first came back? I overheard Dematith ask you about it. And I heard you answer him. You said it was in our wigwam. That was a lie, Mishbee. When I went inside, I didn't see the pendant anywhere. I notice these things, and it doesn't make any sense to me. The only thing I can be sure of is that you're keeping a secret."

Mishbee didn't want to tell Oobata everything, but she had to tell her something. If she wasn't truthful, Oobata would know. "I was thinking about the winter feasts, Oobata. I was distracted and didn't work as hard as

I should have in the woods today ..."

Just then Mishbee was interrupted. Her father flew into camp, breathless and agitated. He was a respected hunter and an elder in their small coastal hunting group. Although Mishbee was thankful that she didn't have to finish her story, it was obvious that something was terribly wrong. The women, the few children, and all the men instinctively gathered around Mishbee's father. The group felt terror settle over them, and everything seemed to go suddenly still. When Mishbee's father caught his breath enough to speak, he told them what he had seen. "When I was in the woods, I spotted settlers hunting in the bush just east of our encampment."

Mishbee gulped. Her father had seen John! This man who had loved and protected her all her life had seen her secret. But that couldn't be. Obviously, her father hadn't seen her speaking to John or he would have said something to her by now.

Mishbee's father continued his story. "At least two of them had muskets. Our land is being taken once again. The *aichmudyim* has returned! We're no longer safe here. The council must meet. We must hurry." Mishbee's father spoke of the white men as the devil.

In the summer the tribe broke up into small hunting groups of a dozen and a half or so people. But even so a small council was formed to be consulted with before the group made a decision. This was an emergency and there was no time to waste.

With memories of the death of Mishbee's cousin still fresh in their minds, the council people didn't take long to decide to move the camp the next morning. The thunderous noise of the musket, the death, the ceremony, the ochre, the birchbark, all of it was etched into their memories as if it happened yesterday. They didn't want anything to do with the settlers.

Mishbee crawled into her sleeping nook beside Oobata. The smoke-filled wigwam provided light protection from the summer weather. She curled up in her spruce boughs, but it was useless. That night sleep wasn't restful for Mishbee. Visions of the settler boy haunted her weary mind. Every time she reached the brink of sleep, she jerked awake as if she were once again staring into the barrel of his musket. She could never tell her father what had happened today. He would never forgive her carelessness. He had loved his nephew as if he were his own son. The grief was too fresh in his mind.

Early the next morning the group gathered up the few tools, skins, and food in order to abandon their campsite. Mishbee hated to leave, but she was used to this nomadic way of life. Every season they followed their food supply.

"You had an uneasy sleep," Oobata said. "It was as if something were frightening you awake every hour."

"I'm worried about the settlers," Mishbee answered truthfully.

Every summer they came to the coast to hunt birds and fish and gather eggs. But the coast was quickly becoming dotted with the settlers' communities, making it more difficult for Mishbee's people to access their coastal lifeline.

After everything was packed, Mishbee's people huddled together with all their earthly possessions to plan their trip. "I saw them inland a little to the east," Mishbee's father said. "We should head west."

The elders of the tiny council agreed, and the group

decided to move westward along the coast. It was still too early to go inland where they lived during the winter, and hopefully there wasn't a new settlement of the foreigners to the west.

The wigwams were left behind, but they would build new ones. The group headed down to the water and into their large canoes. Mishbee remembered watching her father and mother make their canoe. The Beothuks' canoes were quite different from the settlers' boats. They were long and had high, curved fronts and backs to protect their occupants from the ocean spray. The canoes didn't have flat bottoms. Instead the two sides came straight up from the centre, giving the vessels a lot of depth for the unpredictable ocean waters. Rocks were placed in the centre to provide balance and moss was used to provide comfortable upholstery.

To make a canoe, Mishbee's father stripped sheets of birchbark from the trees, and her mother sewed the pieces together to form a single sheet. Later the birchbark sheet was put on the ground and a piece of spruce was placed in the centre to form a frame. The bark had to be folded to make the sides of the canoe. Then her father strengthened the vessel with tapered poles of spruce, which her mother latched to the bark with split spruce roots. Finally, her father put crossbars in the middle to hold the canoe sides open. Mishbee recalled helping to waterproof the boat with a thick coating of heated tree gum, charcoal, and red ochre.

Now this canoe would save their lives. A half-dozen people climbed into her family's canoe. The women and children huddled in the middle where the sides extended much wider and higher than the rest of the vessel.

"I haven't forgotten what we talked about yesterday," Oobata said quietly into Mishbee's ear.

Mishbee wished that Oobata *would* forget.

The canoes and paddlers were efficient. Mishbee loved and feared the ocean all at the same time. It gave them food and travel, but it could also be angry and unpredictable. A great monster lived in the sea, and it was important to respect and not disturb that creature.

Travel was easy today, and they found a suitable site about an hour later in a quiet inlet. After unloading, they quickly busied themselves by building the cone-shaped summer wigwams.

A few of the younger women started digging out a round pit, slightly lower than ground level. The centre of this structure would become the fireplace. The men quickly cut down and gathered birch trees for the frame of the wigwam. Mishbee loved to latch these birch poles together. Many found it difficult, but it was one of her special talents. She was pleased as she worked skilfully and quickly. Oobata helped her, but she wasn't as good as Mishbee. As the two sisters worked, Mishbee's father cut birch trees and her mother attended the fire.

Oobata seized this quiet moment for conversation. "Mishbee, you can't keep secrets from me. The spirits won't allow it. I'm your only sister! You have to tell me what happened yesterday."

"Won't you give up, Oobata?"

"No, I won't. Not until you tell me your secret."

Mishbee continued to latch the poles together. Their conversation stopped abruptly when Demratith returned with yet another pole. Impatiently, they waited for him to leave.

Mishbee glanced around to see if anyone was close. "Oobata, the spirits want me to be quiet," she hissed.

"I was right. Something *did* happen. Tell me, tell me!"

"No, Oobata, I can't. As I said before, the spirits want me to be quiet."

Oobata reflected for a long moment, then sighed. "If the spirits want you to be quiet, you must do as they say."

"Thank you, Oobata," Mishbee said, relieved.

"Let's go get more birchbark."

The two set out to gather layers of birchbark to tile over the wigwam. This natural shingling would protect them from the weather. Mishbee looked around as they walked about their new camp collecting bark. The rocky coastline was very rugged, and the icy ocean melted into an ominous grey sky.

When they returned, they carefully layered the bark over the frame with their mother. Oobata added some skins and furs to the exterior, leaving only a small hole at the top over the fire hole. When they were finished, the girls went inside their newly created structure to inspect it.

"It looks good," Oobata said.

"Yes, it is good," Mishbee said. "I like our new home."

"We're good building partners."

Mishbee smiled at her sister. "And good friends."

It was hard to believe that this small group of people could construct this temporary home in little more than an hour.

Mishbee went back outside to gather firewood and

some tree boughs. She dug out a fire pit in the centre of the wigwam, then scooped out a little hollow for herself to sleep in. Mishbee lined the hole with several boughs and a caribou skin. She was looking forward to curling up in her new bed tonight.

They finished setting up the new camp just in time. The sky grew quite dark, and before long rain fell in great sheets. Lightning illuminated the sky and the thunder spoke. The small band of people eagerly took refuge inside their wigwams.

"When the sky is blue, it's bluer than the sea," Oobata said to Mishbee, "but when it's grey, it's truly dismal."

Mishbee heard the pelting rain hit the birchbark exterior. She was grateful that her father had already started a fire in the centre of the wigwam.

"Yes, it's certainly a dismal night outside," Mishbee said. But it wasn't dismal inside the wigwam. She stared at the flickering fire as the flames danced and cast warm shadows on the faces of her family. She didn't care that it was pouring outside. The past two days had been long and tiring for her. The hours had been filled with hard work, terror, and travel. It was a great relief just to sit around the fire in the comfort of her family's shelter.

Mishbee's mother had taken a cormorant that her father had caught and skewered it to roast it on the fire. Mishbee took some of the berries she had picked the day before and ate them with the pieces of flesh off the bird. It felt good to eat, good to be here, and good to be alive.

"Mishbee," her father said as soon as they finished their supper, "you worked well today. I'm proud of you."

"Thank you, Father," she said, pleased with herself.

"You're a good girl."

That night Mishbee curled up into a very contented ball. Unlike the previous evening, she closed her eyes and slept well.

CHAPTER 4

*B*ang, Bang! The distant sound of hammering echoed through John's once-sleeping body. He had only been on Exploits Island for a little over two weeks and already he despised waking up to the sound of hammering in the middle of the night. It meant only one thing.

A deep chill overtook him as he stumbled out of bed to find his pocket watch. The moon was bright, and he was able to read the time by the window. "One o'clock," he mumbled to himself, shaking his head and slowly crawling back into bed. There was nothing he could do except listen to the ominous pounding ring throughout the cove. John didn't know how long it went on, but finally the incessant din stopped. However, he didn't find any comfort in the silence. It simply meant the coffin must be finished.

Finally, John drifted back into a fitful sleep, only to be awakened by the sound of voices coming from the common room. He had obviously overslept. Elizabeth Manuel's friend Gertie was over for tea.

"How's the boy making out, Lizzie?" he heard Gertie ask.

"Oh, not too bad, dear. It's been a lot for him. You know he's only fifteen, and making that long voyage across the ocean alone all the way from Yarmouth for someone his age is no picnic, I'm sure. I think he misses his father and sister. It's my understanding they were very close. Can I get you more tea?" Elizabeth offered.

"What about his mother?"

"Oh, she passed on a few years back. It's a shame for a youngster to grow up without a mother. She was a distant relative of my husband Joseph's, you know. It was only proper that we offer to bring him over here and teach him a trade at his father's request. Joseph says the young lad has a real talent with wood. He'll be a good apprentice building those schooners, and Joseph can use all the help he can get. This island is no longer a little fishing stop anymore. Each passing day since Joseph and his brothers, Samuel and William, decided to settle here year-round, more and more people have also decided to stay and make a go of it. We're only a handful of families right now, but I dare say that in a couple of years Exploits will be a regular little establishment."

Gertie chuckled. "Yes, 'tis true. I can hardly believe we stayed last winter. Fred has a way of convincing me of these things. However, many o' days I miss England!"

"Speaking about youngsters without mothers, it's a crying shame about Maud last night. Poor little Sarah and Annie. They'll be bringing each other up now, I suppose. That's a pity — youngsters raising themselves."

"Yes, it certainly is. And poor Allen. As if he hasn't been through enough losing a brother to them savages. And now a sister to disease."

John instantly thought of Mishbee. How could she be a *savage*? He was relieved that the ladies were no longer talking about him but devastated that the coffin being built in the middle of the night was for Allen's sister, Maud. John quickly washed and dressed. He had to find his friend.

However, John couldn't escape breakfast. Mrs. Manuel fussed and made him sit at the table for tea, bread and butter, and a hardboiled egg for strength. He looked at her closely as she busied herself in the kitchen. She didn't look like the women in Yarmouth with their perfectly styled hair and smart and tidy clothes. The porcelain complexions of England were replaced with rough, weathered skin, tough hands from hard labour, and greying hair barely kept under control. It was a different kind of beauty. It was the beauty of strength and fortitude. It wasn't worn on the outside like a fancy hat, but rather, on the inside like a permanent badge of courage.

When he finished breakfast, John stepped outside. Joseph Manuel would be down by the dock or at the lumber yard or maybe catching fish for this evening's supper. It seemed impossible that only yesterday he had met Mishbee and only last night Maud had died. Both events seemed lifetimes apart. It didn't feel right that the sun was shining so brightly and that the ocean sparkled so beautifully. He took a moment to scan the scenery of this new island home where he had already begun to sink tentative roots into. From the inner harbour he could see the rocky hills that made up this harsh landscape. A dozen or so wooden homes peppered the shoreline randomly, decorating the desolate land with spurts of colour.

Several docks protruded into the ocean. Although minor intrusions in this vast expanse of water, these docks housed the essential transportation the settlers needed for survival. As John walked up the hill towards Allen's house, he passed the graveyard and then several fishing nets set out for mending. The smell of smoke wafting from chimneys was mixed with the odours of fish and salt air.

Maud's body was laid out in the front room of Allen's house. Allen looked sullen when John entered. Edgar, Maud's husband, and their two young girls, Sarah and Annie, stared blankly at the coffin.

"I'm sorry, Allen," John said.

"Yes, well, it's a cruel world, isn't it?"

"Yes, 'tis that." John's eyes flickered to Annie, the youngest girl sitting in the room. He had seen her only two days ago running around on the paths of the island, singing and playing with endless energy and spirit. He thought of his own mother's funeral only four years earlier. The pain only seemed stronger now as he witnessed this scene.

Suddenly, Allen fixed John with an angry glare and spat out, "Those blasted Indians took my brother and now *this*. It isn't fair, John. It isn't fair."

John didn't know what to say, so he said nothing. He simply stayed next to his friend offering silent sympathy. When more people arrived, John returned home to the Manuels' place.

That afternoon he helped Mrs. Manuel stack wood. He was happy to do an easy task that kept his mind off the events of the past day. Once the woodpile was finished, John decided to go for a walk to clear his head. He followed the path up over the hill and noticed someone familiar sitting down and staring out at the ocean.

"Hello, Annie," he said.

"Hello," she said warily. "How do you know my name?"

The nine-year-old viewed John with suspicion. Her face was a combination of sadness and anger.

"I'm new here, but I'm good friends with your Uncle Allen."

"Oh," Annie said, her glower subsiding a little.

John studied the girl's tousled chestnut-brown hair and her tear-stained cheeks, which seemed more freckles than face.

"What are you doing up here on this path?" she asked.

"Just going for a walk. I had a lot on my mind."

"Me, too." She sighed heavily. "They're burying my mother in a couple of hours."

"I'm sorry."

"Me, too. She was very sick. My father says at least she isn't suffering anymore, but I'm still sad."

"And so you should be."

Annie turned and shot John a piercing look. "And how would you know how I should feel? Did you ever lose a mother?"

John cleared his throat. "Yes, I did. And I wasn't much older than you are now when my mother died. Except I lived in England then."

"Oh …" Annie said. "What's it like living without a mother?"

"Well, it isn't easy, but I still have memories of her. I try to be strong for her. And I had my older sister to help me. It hurt really bad at first. Over time I learned to keep going, though. That's why I came here to Exploits Island — to make a new life for myself, to keep going."

"Yes, that's what my father says. He says we have to keep going somehow. He also says I talk too much, so I don't know if I believe him. You don't think I chatter on too much, do you?"

John chuckled. "No, no, you don't talk too much at all. But your father's right about the other matter. For your mother's sake you have to keep going. Annie, we should head back now for your mother's burial."

Annie's face darkened. "I'm not going."

John was shocked by her response. "Annie, you must come. You can't miss your own mother's burial!"

"And why not?"

"Because it's your mother. It's only proper you should be there to say goodbye."

"I don't want to say goodbye."

"But you have to … you should —"

"No!" Annie shouted.

John saw how determined Annie was, so he took a different approach. "I see. I guess it's your decision. Well, if you aren't coming, I guess I'll be leaving." John stood and pretended he was making the journey down to the graveyard. He was careful not to look back.

It seemed like forever, but finally she called out, "Wait!"

He stopped in his tracks and turned around. "I'll wait."

Annie stood, brushed the dirt off her clothes, and ran towards John. "Would you stand beside me at the burial? Would you?"

"Of course I will," he told her.

The two made their way to the cemetery, and John watched as Edgar, Allen, Sarah, and Annie said their final goodbyes to Maud. The scene only brought back bad memories of his own mother's funeral. He wanted to run away and escape it all but instead remained there for Annie and for Allen.

After the burial, John returned to the Manuels' house. When supper was finished, Joseph invited John to sit and socialize with him and his wife, but John wanted to be alone. "Thank you, Mr. Manuel, but I'm very tired. I think I'll write a letter to my sister and go to bed early tonight."

Elizabeth Manuel nodded. "As you will. It's been a full day."

"That it has," John muttered to himself as he went to his bedroom.

Sitting at the table in his room, John chided himself for not having written his sister since his arrival. A letter from him was well overdue. He took a few moments to think, then wrote:

Dearest Ruth,

I'm sorry it has taken me so long to write. Settling into this new land and getting my bearings has taken its toll and time. My thoughts are with you and Father and I often think of the docks at Yarmouth.

The crossing was terrible. The Atlantic is a huge ocean, and I was sick the entire time. I'm glad to finally be here. However, it is much harsher than I ever anticipated. I can tell that I can make something of myself here. I have discovered that I don't care much for hunting, but I'm a splendid carpenter. Father knows me well and knew this was where I could fulfill my dreams to be a shipbuilder. He must have watched me all those days as a youngster as I stared at the ships in Yarmouth Harbour.

Mother's distant cousin, Joseph, is a good man, and he and his wife treat me well. I won't be totally engaged in schooner building until the winter months, and I'm looking forward to that time. I've found a friend in a young man named Allen. He's a few years older than I am but has proven to be good company nonetheless.

I've met a variety of people here, all interesting in their own way. The newness of this land never ceases to amaze me. Every day is an unbelievable adventure, sometimes filled with sadness as well as mystery. Give my love to Father and tell him I look at the pocket watch every time I get lonely.

Regards,
John

John carefully read over the letter, then folded it. He wanted to tell his sister about Mishbee, the mysterious new stranger he had encountered, but he knew telling her about Indians would only cause her to worry about his safety. John walked over to his bedroom window. The wind had picked up speed and brought in a sudden rain-storm. John could barely make out the ocean through the torrents of rain. He gazed out at the unpredictable sea with its angry waves crashing against the rugged coast. Was it only yesterday that he had travelled with Allen from this little island to the big island of Newfoundland? It seemed so far away now. Was it only a day earlier that he had chanced upon Mishbee? A twig hit the window-pane, making a methodical *tap, tap* that merged with the pounding rain on the glass.

Where was Mishbee now? Was she safely out of this storm? Would their chance meeting ever occur again? Today he had dealt with death and the trials of living. What were Mishbee and her people coping with? Too many questions haunted him, and there was no way to find easy answers. In fact, the only person he could safely direct these questions to was himself. Judging by Allen's bitter response this afternoon, he knew he could never speak about Mishbee to anyone here.

Summer would soon be over. The violent storm out-side seemed to announce as much. John sighed heavily and went to bed.

CHAPTER 5

"Get up," Oobata said, shaking Mishbee.

Was it morning already? Mishbee wondered. "Go away, Oobata," she moaned, trying to escape her sister's jostling. She pushed at Oobata, hoping her sister would stop annoying her, but it didn't work.

Oobata continued to prod and poke Mishbee. "Don't be so lazy. It's time to get up."

"I know, I know." Reluctantly, Mishbee crawled out from her cozy spot in the wigwam and followed her sister outside. Summer had turned to fall, and she could see her breath in the cool air. Mishbee stretched on tiptoe. "It's getting colder every day."

Oobata nodded and smiled knowingly in agreement. Mishbee stretched again and turned to look at the wigwam. Frost had settled on the earth. They could no longer drive the supporting birch poles of their homes into the ground as they usually did. Instead, rocks were piled to make a circular base so that the birch logs could then be wedged in between, thus avoiding digging into the harder soil.

"We've got a lot to do today, Mishbee," Oobata said. "I overheard Father talking last night."

"What is it?" Mishbee asked worriedly.

"The days are getting shorter and the temperature is falling. I heard Father say we'll start heading inland today."

Mishbee was so excited she could hardly contain herself. This meant they would soon join the rest of their tribe and plan for the caribou hunt.

"What are we waiting for, Oobata? Let's get started!" Mishbee was ready to gather her things and begin the journey that very minute.

"Shh!" Oobata grabbed Mishbee's arm. "Don't be so impulsive. We must wait for Father to announce this. Otherwise he'll know that I overheard him."

Mishbee didn't want to wait, but she knew Oobata was right. Going inland meant winter was just around the corner. Despite its cold harshness, winter was a time of festivities and families. Mishbee loved being reunited with her entire tribe of more than a hundred people. It was always fascinating to listen to everything the other bands had experienced during the summer.

"Mishbee," her mother called out, interrupting her thoughts, "help me with this fire."

Dutifully, Mishbee assisted her mother with the food preparations. It wasn't long before the rest of the band was awake and preparing breakfast. Then Mishbee's father called everyone together.

"I think it's time to head back," he said. "The weather is changing quickly, and the caribou will be running soon. We need to be home in time for the hunt."

Dematith and a few others readily agreed. There was little time for talk. The next few days would be dedicated to trekking upriver to the interior. Mishbee and Oobata quickly gathered their furs and some food. As she left her wigwam, Mishbee didn't look back. Unlike her, the wigwam would go through the winter alone and empty.

The trip was exhausting, but it was worth the effort. Mishbee's heartbeat quickened as she entered the interior village a few days later. It was dusk and still light enough to get a good look at her familiar home. It was obvious that their summer hunting group was the last one to return.

Mishbee spotted Chief Statuon, who stood in the centre of the village near the smokehouse talking to several people, his striking red ochre staff in hand. The chief was known for his great ability to hunt and for his leadership skills. Mishbee admired the beautiful half-moon bone carving sparkling on the end of the chief's spectacular sceptre.

As Mishbee headed to her family's *mamateek*, she was pleased to see that the dwelling had lasted the entire summer unscathed. The multi-sided, sturdy wooden structure housed twenty people. Mishbee also noted the racks filled with dried fish, salmon, lobster tails, and bladders of seal oil. It was obvious that the summer had been good for all of her people, and the caribou meat was yet to be harvested. This would be a bountiful winter. Mishbee scanned the arrows and prized possessions that lined the walls of the *mamateek*. Her thoughts were interrupted when Oobata walked into the dwelling.

"It's good to be back, isn't it, Mishbee?"

"Yes, Oobata, it certainly is." Mishbee released a happy sigh. She was relieved to be back home for another fall and winter.

"We should go now," Oobata said.

Mishbee faced her sister. "What is it?"

"It's time to join the others. Everyone has gathered around the fire. The chief is going to speak tonight."

Without hesitation Mishbee followed Oobata to the village centre. Once around the fire, the entire tribe would feast and sing songs about darkness, mountains, ice, caribou, and fire. Some would carve while others played games. All would listen to the stories. It was a time when both children and elders sat together enjoying one another's company.

Mishbee leaned close to Oobata. "I think Chief Statuon is going to tell a story soon."

She was right. The chief's voice carried over all the people. "It is time," he began, "to tell the young ones of our tribe's beginnings."

The tribe immediately hushed in collective anticipation. Mishbee snuggled a little closer to Oobata. She loved the stories and myths that each generation passed on to the next.

"A long time ago the world was empty of people."

Mishbee noticed that Dematith was carving another bone pendant by the firelight as he listened to the chief.

"Our people did not roam the rocks, brooks, or sea," the chief continued. "The Voice told us that things were not always as they are today. Before the settlers, before our people, a Great Arrow came from the sky."

Mishbee spotted a new baby in the tribe this autumn. The tiny girl wriggled as the mother held her prize tenderly. Mishbee recognized the little girl's older brother. Newborn children represented hope for a promising future. Mishbee whispered quietly enough to Oobata so as not to disturb Chief Statuon's story. "What is the new baby's name?"

"She's called Shanawdithit," Oobata said.

"Ah," Mishbee said reflectively.

"From this Great Arrow," the chief told them, "we sprang forth to inhabit this land, to respect this earth, and to live with its bounty. We were here first, but many were to follow. The first foreign settlers to come were of the Good Spirit. They came to make peace with our people and to bring gifts. But, as my father has passed on to me and his father before him, the next settlers to come were of the Bad Spirit. They came only to destroy and take from our people. They played tricks on us and hurt us."

Mishbee began to feel uncomfortable. John had spared her life. He couldn't have been of the Bad Spirit, could he? She wished she could tell the chief that not all of the settlers were of the Bad Spirit, that some were good. Well, at least one was, or so she hoped.

"Children," the chief continued, "when your time comes for the final sleep, you will go to the country of the Good Spirit. It is a happy island where one can hunt and fish and feast. It is far away, where the sun goes down behind the mountains in the west."

The chief was finished his story, and the night's festivities drew to an end. It was time for sleep. Mishbee curled up in her spruce-and-fur-lined hollow in the *mamateek*. She couldn't fall asleep right away, though. Her mind kept replaying the chief's words: *The next settlers to come were of the Bad Spirit ... The next settlers to come were of the Bad Spirit ...*

When Mishbee awakened early the next morning from her fitful sleep, she knew it was time to put on her caribou leggings and wrap, for it was quickly becoming cold. She busied herself tending the fire when all of a

43

sudden a thunderous cry rang through the village. Fear gripped her as she recognized Dematith's voice. Why was he yelling? What was wrong? Were settlers invading their quiet village? Quickly, she ran to find out.

Dematith shouted once again, this time more clearly. "The *osweet* are here! They're running. The caribou hunt is on!"

The village buzzed with organized confusion. Men ran to grab their spears. Others were already on their way to the hunt, while another group ran to watch the annual hunt.

"Let's go see," Oobata said, snatching Mishbee's hand as they ran furiously up the hill to the lookout over the river. From this vantage point both hunter and beast would be in clear view. Every year many spectators gathered there during the hunt to observe the collective, organized effort of gathering food.

"If this hunt is good, the winter will be good," Oobata mused as they gazed upon the huge, running animals from their perch on the hill.

"The winter will be good, anyway," Mishbee added. "You're getting married to Dematith!"

Oobata smiled. "Yes, you're right. It will be a good winter."

Every year the hunting groups that returned earliest from the summer felled hundreds of trees to create endless miles of fences by the river so that the caribou could cross the water in only a few spots between the blockades of trees and poles. Once the caribou were driven into the water, they were easily speared by the waiting hunters.

Mishbee watched as the men made loud noises to scare the caribou into the water. There men waited in canoes with their spears poised. They could canoe faster than the mighty animals could swim. Mishbee always marvelled at the grace and ease of these magnificent creatures and was eternally thankful for them. Survival would be difficult, if not impossible, without the skins, meat, bones, and antlers of this worshipped animal. Reverence and respect were duly given these life-giving beasts.

The men carried the many carcasses back to camp. It was important that they follow the *tabus*, the ritual, so the caribou spirit wouldn't be offended. All worked very hard after such a hunt. There was no time to spare.

"Help me skin this hide, Mishbee," Oobata commanded.

Mishbee took a tool made of bone and started to scrape the flesh from the skin. Oobata moved closer to Mishbee and spoke in a hushed tone so the other women couldn't hear them. "Do the spirits tell you to be silent still?"

Although it had been a long time since they had last spoken of that summer day Mishbee had returned late from the woods, Mishbee knew exactly what her sister was talking about. Mishbee continued to work, trying not to make eye contact with Oobata. She cleared her throat and remained firm in her resolve. "I must remain quiet, Oobata. I can't share the secret."

"The wind tells me otherwise, Mishbee," Oobata said, scraping at the caribou skin. "But I'll trust you. You give me no other choice."

Deep down Mishbee wanted to tell Oobata about John, the settler. It was difficult for her to keep this secret from her sister, but the chief's stories were fresh in her mind. She was still too fearful and wary to share her experience.

There were few women in the village who could cure skins as well as Mishbee. She took pride in carefully and patiently rubbing and pounding the skins with a rock until they became pliable and supple. Sometimes it was necessary to chew spots until Mishbee was finally satisfied with the texture. She loved the smell and texture of the soft, warm fur. She enjoyed rubbing her hands along the nap of the perfect hair, feeling its thick warmth. Taking these skins and furs and transforming them into warm, protective garments was a task that brought Mishbee great joy.

Much of the caribou meat had to be cut into strips and placed in the smokehouse. This building contained lattice-work shelves and large openings in the walls to allow the air and smoke to circulate freely around the meat. Once the meat was dried it would no longer spoil and would be ready to eat.

Since the caribou run was so plentiful this year, it was also necessary to prepare some of the meat for freezing. The bones were removed, and the villagers packed the meat in large spruce bark boxes with the hearts and tongues always placed in the middle. When the frost set in, the meat would keep. Some of it was put in storehouses and the rest was placed in pits lined with birchbark in the nearby forest.

It took days to complete the work, but when everything was done it was time for the great feast. Mishbee sat in the *mamateek* and watched Oobata put on her new mantle made of otter. "It's beautiful, Oobata."

"And warm, too," her sister said, stroking the otter fur. "It's time for the celebrations. Let's go."

The two headed towards the fire where the tribe had assembled for the ceremonies. Several antlers had been placed on the projecting rocks on the bank of the river.

"We are here to honour the *osweet* who give us life," the chief began. "We do not offend you, oh, spirits, we thank you."

After the chief was finished, the tribe sang songs about the mighty caribou. Then a fine powder was passed around to everyone in the group. Mishbee cupped her hand to take some of the dust to feast on. Many of the caribou bones had been boiled and the marrow had been ground to make this special delicacy for tonight's celebrations. No part of the caribou was wasted.

Mishbee noticed Dematith staring at Oobata. Soon they would be married, and it would be time for another celebration!

When the evening's festivities were over, it was very late. Oobata and Mishbee walked back to their *mamateek.*

"Look, Oobata," Mishbee said, pointing at the illuminated sky, "the spirit of the *osweet* is dancing!"

Above them the northern lights shimmered.

"It's beautiful," Oobata said. "I guess the spirits are pleased."

The girls sat outside the *mamateek* in silence and watched the spectacular display of colour and movement. When the colours subsided, the girls went inside the *mamateek* to nestle into their warm spruce bough beds. Sleep came almost instantly.

The next morning Mishbee helped her mother make breakfast. When she went outside to get more wood for the fire, she saw that her father didn't look well. He seemed to walk slowly and stiffly.

"What's wrong, Father?" Mishbee asked.

"I'm getting older and the hunt is getting harder on my body. I'm just tired, Mishbee."

Mishbee could tell by the way her father walked that his body ached. She knew immediately what would help him. "I'll prepare you a sweat bath, Father."

"Thank you, my child. That would be good."

Mishbee went to the water's edge to find the best rocks suitable for the pile she needed. Next she gathered small twigs and branches to start a fire over the rocks. During the day, Mishbee allowed the fire to burn until it smouldered into ash. Then she carefully cleaned the ash from the fire, leaving only hot, clean rocks.

"Father, it's ready," she announced.

Wearily, her father squatted over the still-warm rocks as Mishbee doused them with water. When the steam began to rise, she covered her father with a birchbark canopy. Hot steam remained inside the makeshift sauna to penetrate the aches, pains, and chills that afflicted her father. He sat there for quite a while, enjoying the heat that suffused his muscles.

Afterward Mishbee's father felt better and lay down in the *mamateek* to sleep. He appeared content and comfortable and was back to his usual self the next day.

"Mishbee, you're a good girl," her father said to her at breakfast. "I feel much better today. I'm ready to go out and hunt another fifty caribou."

Of course, Mishbee knew her father was joking. He wouldn't be hunting another fifty caribou! Still, it was nice to be appreciated. "Thank you, Father."

"Someday in the near future you'll make someone a good wife."

Mishbee was taken aback by her father's comment and felt a little embarrassed. She hadn't thought about getting married before. She had focused so much on Oobata's wedding that she had never even considered the fact that in the next few years she would be ready for marriage herself.

Her father seemed to read her thoughts. "But there's plenty of time to decide about marriage later."

Plenty of time, Mishbee thought. If there was one thing she and her people had, it was plenty of time.

Chapter 6

John desperately wanted to wipe the sawdust and bits of wood from his eyes. The itchy flakes of timber fell like snowflakes from above.

"Good work there, John!" Joseph Manuel shouted down. "We're almost done this plank. I must say, it's a beauty. Straight as a pin, it is!"

John was relieved to hear that the end was in sight. His arms and shoulders ached as he continued with the push and pull of the two-man saw. He and Joseph had taken turns being the "low men" of the saw pit because it was the worst job. Standing below meant sawdust showers and sore arms.

Joseph had built the saw pit himself. Its construction involved digging a pit six feet deep, four feet wide, and six feet long. A log that was to be cut was placed on a platform on top of the pit and moved forward on rollers as it was sawn. One man stood in the pit and worked the narrow end of the saw, while the other man stood above the pit, guiding the blade along a line on the log made by dipping a length of twine in ochre and snapping it against the top side of the log to create a straight line.

"Hold up, John!" Joseph cried. "We're done!"

John felt the tension of the saw release, quickly wiped

his eyes, and took off his hat to shake his hair. Despite the hard manual labour that sawing timber involved, John loved the fragrant scent of the freshly cut wood.

"Time to go home!" Joseph yelled over the noise of the other men who were constructing the covered platform where Joseph's blueprints for the schooner would be kept.

"As you say," Mr. Lily, one of the other men hollered back. "Good night, Joseph."

As they headed back to the Manuels' house, John felt his muscles hurt a bit more when he and Joseph passed the trenches he had dug the day before where the ship's keel would be laid. Building schooners was certainly tough.

Joseph broke the silence. "How are you finding the work, John?"

"I don't think I have any muscles left that aren't aching right now. But despite that, I love working with the wood."

Joseph chuckled. "The aches and pains never really go away. It's hard work, but it's worth it. And you really show promise, John. You should be proud."

John turned crimson at this remark. Embarrassed as he was, though, he truly was pleased with himself.

"I'm expecting the oak to arrive from Nova Scotia any day now for the keel," Joseph said. "Then the real fun begins."

Their conversation was interrupted by the appearance of young Annie. Since the death of her mother, Annie had attached herself to John as if he were a newfound brother.

"Hello, John," she chirped.

"Well, hello there, Annie."

She strolled along with John and Joseph towards the Manuel residence.

"What did you do today, Annie?" Joseph asked.

"Let's see. I did my lessons, I helped Sarah bake some bread, and I visited Uncle Allen."

"Good for you," John said, grinning. "I'm glad to see you're making yourself useful."

"I would have much rather played all day," Annie lamented.

John laughed. "Poor Annie, worked to the bone."

"Yes, that's me," she said dramatically.

Such big woes from such a little girl, John thought.

"It's difficult," Annie added, "but someone has to do it."

They were almost at the Manuel home, and Annie scampered off as quickly as she had arrived.

"Bye," she sang out in a suddenly cheerful voice.

"Goodbye," John called after her.

When John entered the house, Elizabeth Manuel demanded, "What on earth happened to you?"

John was so startled he didn't know what to say.

"Get yourself out of here and shake yourself off!" Elizabeth ordered.

John realized he was shedding wood shavings all over the floor. Apologizing over Joseph's laughter, he went back out to the porch and removed the heavy wool sweater that Elizabeth had knitted for him. When he shook it, he sent bits of wood flying in every direction. Without the sweater on, he shivered slightly in the late fall air, prompting him to duck back into the house swiftly.

The smell of fresh-baked bread filled the kitchen. It was obvious that Elizabeth had been busy all day. She bustled around, serving tea, salt venison, and cabbage for supper. "So, was it a good day at the shipyard?" she asked her husband.

"Yes, quite productive," Joseph said. "Young John here did a good job of being low man in the saw pit."

"I could tell that the second he and all those bits of wood entered the house tonight!"

The three chuckled.

"When's it going to be again, Lizzie?" Joseph asked.

"It's supposed to be another two months, but I feel like it's going to be sooner."

John smiled as he watched the two banter, recalling the day Joseph had told him that Elizabeth was going to have a baby.

"Well, as long as Gertie's nearby, all will be well," Joseph said.

"Yes, I suppose. I'm just glad you aren't winterhousing this year up in that old tilt on the hill. I think I'll need you close by."

"No, I don't need to go inland to get food or wood this winter, my dear. I'll be here."

"Oh, John, I almost forgot!" Elizabeth said. "The mail came today and there's a letter from your family. I left it on your bed."

After they finished eating, John quickly went to his room to read the letter. He could tell by the even, flowing script on the envelope that the letter was from his sister and could hardly contain himself as he ripped it open and read its brief contents:

Dearest John,

I have so much to tell you! I am glad to hear that you are settling in suitably! Father sends his love and is likewise happy to hear you are well. We miss you terribly but know you must chase your dream.

You remember George Nelson, don't you? Of course, you do, I'm sure. Anyway, he has asked me to marry him! Isn't that wonderful? I am so excited, and plans for the wedding are being made. I know that it's unlikely for you to return for the event, but I wanted you to know.

Much love,
Ruth

John folded the letter carefully and got his carving knife from the drawer in his dresser. Then he picked up a piece of pine and headed to the kitchen to sit by the fire with the Manuels. Elizabeth was knitting, and Joseph was smoking his pipe, enjoying the quiet evening.

"So what news is there back in England, John?" Elizabeth asked.

"My sister, Ruth, is engaged to be married!"

"Well, I declare, that's wonderful! Do you know the gentleman she's marrying?"

"Yes, I know him well. His name is George Nelson and he's a good man."

"Ah, that's nice, very nice."

"Yes, it is," John said. Secretly, though, he felt

a little sad knowing he wouldn't be there for her wedding, wouldn't see her joy or be able to congratulate the groom. But he didn't share his dismay with the Manuels. Instead, he started to carve, something he always found relaxing.

"Are you carving again?" Elizabeth asked. "I don't understand why you do that after a full day of working in the wood yard! Sometimes you don't make any sense to me."

John had heard this speech many times before and had learned to ignore Elizabeth's mild chastisement. However, he didn't have time to get far with the carving of his new pendant, for there was a knock on the door. When John looked up, Allen was entering the house, hat in hand.

"Good evening, Mr. and Mrs. Manuel, John," Allen said.

"Welcome!" the Manuels said in unison.

"Hello, Allen," John greeted his friend.

Elizabeth quickly put water on to boil for tea and began cutting slabs of bread for the guest.

"How's the schooner building going, John?" Allen asked.

Joseph cut in before John could respond. "Fine, Allen. John's doing an excellent job."

Allen smiled. "Good to hear, good to hear. John, I think I'm going to go winterhousing this year on the main island. There's a trap line I'm thinking of managing."

"You're certainly a good hunter," John said, thinking suddenly of that summer day in the woods when he encountered Mishbee.

Elizabeth served them all tea, and Allen helped himself to a piece of bread and butter, then said, "Yes, I was thinking of setting up a tilt near that pond where we were last summer. I'd like to build it early before the snow comes. Since you're such an expert with an axe, I thought maybe you'd like to come along for a few days and set up camp. Young Noel Paul might stay with me."

John's heart skipped a beat. Would Mishbee still be there? And worse, would Allen stumble upon her while on one of his trapping routes? John couldn't bear the thought of such a misfortune. "I'd love to go," he blurted before remembering he was obliged to work for Joseph. "That is if it's all right with you, Joseph."

"I suppose I could spare you for a few days, but not much longer." Joseph winked. "I've become quite dependent on you, John."

"All right, it's settled," Allen said. "I'll come get you tomorrow at noon, John. Bring your axe and an adze, would you? We're going to need them to build the tilt. Oh, and you'll need warm clothes. We're on the brink of winter. I can feel it. Well, I better go. Thank you for the tea and bread, Mrs. Manuel. Good night, John, Joseph."

"Good night, Allen," John and Joseph both said.

John excused himself to go to bed, but he didn't sleep. He didn't think he would get another chance to look for Mishbee until the spring. The weather was getting colder every day, and the crossing from Exploits to the main island of Newfoundland was no longer as easily negotiated. Also there was no reason to go over to the main island this time of year. There were no more berries, no more trout, and no more summer hunting. There were very few permanent settlers inland, only the occasional trapper and settler cutting wood.

John decided he had to find out if Mishbee was still in the area. If she was, he would have to warn her of the danger. There was no doubt in his mind that he had to keep Allen away from her. Her life depended on it.

When Allen came to pick up John the next day, he had another man with him. "John, I'd like you to meet my new trapping partner, young Noel Paul."

"Hello," John said.

"Hello," the man greeted with reserve.

"Noel is part Micmac and part English," Allen explained. "He knows the woods better than any of us. He's agreed to stay in the tilt with me and help me set up my trapping line. Isn't that great, John?"

John tried to appear enthusiastic, but it was difficult. His worry about Mishbee had only increased. He knew the Micmac and Mishbee's people, the Red Indians, as the settlers called them, were the worst of enemies.

The crossing was cold, and the three men remained silent the whole time. When they arrived on the main island and were soon approaching the pond, John's apprehension grew in leaps and bounds. As soon as they got to their destination, John, Allen, and Noel started chopping trees and stumps to create the makeshift winter tilt — a small one-room cabin made with vertical logs.

By evening they had a decent frame erected and all three could just barely lie inside the new building. They hadn't gathered the stones to build a fireplace yet, so they lit a campfire about a yard away. Noel spoke English well enough but wasn't much of a conversationalist. He went off to gather spruce boughs to put underneath them to protect them from the cold earth. When the young

Micmac returned, they all settled down to enjoy the fire and plan the next day.

"We've got a fair amount to do still," Allen said, "and I'd like to at least scout out a possible trapping route. I suppose we could get the platform for the bed built and finish the walls tomorrow. What do you think, Noel?"

"With the three of us we could get at least that much done," Noel said. "Maybe we'll even have time enough to scout out a possible trapping route. We'll see."

John's mind raced as he tried to think of something to say that would allow him to go off by himself. "When you two scout out a trapping route, maybe I'll do some exploring."

"No," Noel said firmly, "you can come with us. It's not good for one person to wander around alone this time of year."

"But I've been here in the summer without any problem."

"That may be true, but it was warmer then. What if you slip and fall into the water and get cold? This time of year the weather changes quickly and death can come even quicker."

John's desperation intensified. What could he say now? He turned to Allen. "You know how much I enjoy exploring."

"No," Allen said brusquely, "I'm in charge of you and I need to bring you back in one piece to Mr. Manuel. You'll do as Noel says."

John didn't sleep that night. He wasn't sure if it was due to the biting cold or the incessant worry. The next morning the three had a sparse breakfast and headed out to scout a possible trapping route.

Noel negotiated the woods with more skill and agility than either John or Allen. John quickly lost track of where they had travelled. He no longer knew which ponds they had walked around and which hills they had climbed. Tired and discouraged, they finally stumbled into a clearing, and John jumped back at what he saw.

There, before them, were several wigwams. The framing poles were wedged into a large ring of rocks, and some of the birchbark covering had been torn off the structures. Instinctively, John ran towards the wigwams to warn the inhabitants to flee.

"What are you doing, John?" Allen called after him. "Have you lost your mind?"

At that moment it registered with John that the camp was completely deserted. He stopped running and turned sheepishly to look at Allen and Noel.

"It's an old Red Indian camp," Noel said, spitting on the ground. "I don't like these people. I've killed four already and won't rest until I've killed every one I find."

John felt the hair on the back of his neck bristle. He gulped in disbelief. It took every ounce of control he could muster to maintain his composure and hide his disgust.

"They killed my brother," Allen added. "I hate them, too."

Reeling with disappointment at his friend's comment, John said, "Allen, you shouldn't winterhouse here. What if these … these … savages were to find you on your route? Isn't it dangerous?"

Noel laughed. "Hurt Allen?"

"Yes, hurt Allen. What's so funny about that?"

"You settlers don't know much about anything, do you? The Red Indians are all the way upriver inland.

During the winter, you never run into one out here. They're all snug in the interior. The trapping line will be long over by the time they return to the coast."

John nodded. "I see." He didn't know whether to be furious or relieved. At least Mishbee would be safe from Allen and Noel. But what other challenges did she face? What would her winter be like? Would she have enough food? Would her shelter be warm? John took a second look at the wigwams. Instinctively, he walked over to one and stepped inside.

"What are you doing?" Allen demanded.

"Going inside. Want to come?"

"Not for love or money," Allen snapped. "Hurry up, would you? You and your foolish ways."

It took a moment for John's eyes to adjust to the darkness inside the wigwam. He dimly noted the fire pit in the centre and the hollowed sleeping holes lined with spruce boughs. Sitting on the cold earth, he wondered if Mishbee had ever rested here. "So close but always at a distance," he muttered to himself.

"Let's go!" Allen shouted.

Reluctantly, John took one last look at the interior of the wigwam, then got up and ducked through the doorway into the brighter outside light. This camp seemed like such a solemn place somehow. Almost magical.

The trio headed back to the tilt. There was still work to be done. Normally, John would be tired after all the tramping around he had had done, but even despite the lack of sleep the night before he had newfound energy, happy in the knowledge that Mishbee was safe this winter from at least two enemies.

CHAPTER 7

All the members of the *mamateek* were sleeping soundly except for Mishbee. Today was the day Oobata was to be married. Mishbee had been looking forward to the occasion for a long time, yet now she felt a little sad. She found herself thinking about John, the settler boy she had come across the previous year. Although she dearly loved Oobata, she had always secretly wanted a brother, as well. John was very different from her people, but she sensed he would have made a caring sibling. She believed his spirit was good. After all, he had spared her life and restored her precious pendant.

As Mishbee's thoughts spun in the darkness of the *mamateek*, she suddenly noticed that Oobata had awakened and was peering at her. After today, everything would change. Oobata would no longer sleep beside her, tell her stories, or play games with her. Mishbee felt the pain of losing her sister to Dematith, a sense of loss that filled her soul.

As if sensing Mishbee's growing apprehension, Oobata quietly rose and motioned to Mishbee to follow her outside into the crisp winter early-morning air. "Today I get married," she said as they stretched and shivered in the predawn gloom.

"Yes …" Mishbee said slowly.

"It feels strange, doesn't it?"

"Does it feel strange for you, too?" Mishbee perked up a little at the thought that maybe her sister was feeling the same way she was.

"Yes, in a way. I feel as if I'm leaving you. But you're still my sister, Mishbee. That will never change."

Mishbee studied Oobata. "I know I'll always be your sister, but you're also my friend and helper. You know so much about me and keep my secrets. I'll miss having you by my side."

"I won't be far, Mishbee."

"I know, but it won't be the same."

"True, it won't be the same, but it's the way it's meant to be. One day you, too, will get married. You'll see."

"I suppose so." Mishbee felt the wind shift a little. She waited a moment, then continued with determination. "Oobata, remember when I came back to the summer camp without my berries or pendant?"

"How could I forget? It still bothers me."

"It's time I share the story with you."

"Do the spirits say it's time?"

"Yes, the spirits agree."

"What happened that day, Mishbee?"

"I met a settler in the woods."

"Mishbee, you should have told us!" Oobata exploded. "You could have been killed! We *all* could have been killed! Have you forgotten our cousin?"

"I haven't forgotten our cousin. For a long time I stole away to visit his burial cave and hoped he had gone to the happy island. This was in the front of my mind when I met the settler. Don't accuse me of forgetting!"

Mishbee was hurt by her sister's accusations. "It was a boy with a gun, but he didn't hurt me. He spared my life, filled my berry basket, and repaired my pendant."

"Mishbee," Oobata hissed, "don't you remember what Chief Statuon said? Haven't you seen what's happened to our people, our land? Did you talk to this boy?"

"I have seen and I have heard just as you have, Oobata. But this boy is of the Good Spirit. Remember, Chief Statuon said the first settlers were of the Good Spirit."

"But he isn't one of the first settlers! They're all gone."

"Yes, but this boy's spirit is the same as that of the first settlers. I feel it. He and I didn't speak much, since he doesn't have our language. But I did find out that he calls himself John."

"Mishbee, you're crazy! You should never have spoken with this stranger. He could have followed you back to our camp." Oobata was now visibly angry with her sister. She began to pace.

"Don't be silly, Oobata. No settler could follow me in the woods. Please try to understand."

"Understand what? That you're asking the Bad Spirit to visit us? That you're trying to kill us? What don't I understand, Mishbee?"

"You weren't there, Oobata. Open your mind. Today you'll be married and a new life will begin for you. I'll miss you. I want to tell you what happened, but all you can do is scold me. Please, Oobata, listen. Please."

Oobata stared in disbelief at her sister. Then she softened and sighed. "I don't like this, Mishbee, but tell me what happened. Tell me about your good-spirited settler friend."

"I was in the woods collecting blueberries, and I was thinking about the winter festivities and your upcoming wedding. I was distracted, then found myself blinking into the musket of a settler."

"Mishbee, you should always be alert when you're in the woods alone. You know how dangerous it can be if you're not."

"I know I shouldn't have let myself daydream, but I did. This boy was very fair with many small brown spots across his face. They didn't seem painted on but appeared to sit there naturally as if he were born with them. His eyes were blue like the ocean and his hair was the colour of red ochre mixed with gold."

Oobata's eyes grew wider the more Mishbee described her encounter.

"He pointed the gun at me for a long time, and I thought that I, too, would have to be buried. Strangely, though, he put down his gun and backed away. I still thought he was of the Bad Spirit, so I decided to run. I expected that I would die trying to escape this devil, but I wasn't harmed. As I fled, I dropped the berries, and my pendant caught a tree limb and broke. When Dematith asked about my pendant, I knew I had to go back into the woods and find it."

"You went back to where the settler was?" Oobata asked, incredulous.

"Yes, I went back to the spot where I met the stranger and waited silently behind a tree. On the rock where he had sat was my pendant, now repaired, and the berry basket, which he had half-filled. I picked up these things and once again hid. A little later the boy returned. I wanted to thank him for sparing my life, for repairing my pendant, and for picking the berries. I wanted to thank the Good Spirit for protecting me, so I went up to him and spoke to him. He told me his name, then continued to make noise out of his mouth for a long time. But I don't know what he said. All I know is that he came in peace."

"Mishbee, how can you be so sure? Our chief has said many times that settlers are of the Bad Spirit."

"I know, Oobata, but I also know this boy belongs to the Good Spirit of the very first settlers."

Mishbee looked pleadingly at her sister, and Oobata saw the sincerity and certainty in her sister's eyes. "I sense that you're truthful and I sense that you're right. This boy must have been of the Good Spirit, since he didn't kill you *this* time. But you must be careful. We must keep this a secret between us, Mishbee. No one must know. Our people won't accept what you did. They won't approve, and Chief Statuon will be very angry."

"You're right, Oobata. Only you hold my secret."

"Not only is this the day I give the oath of my wedding, but it's also the day I give my oath of secrecy to you."

People were beginning to stir, and the first weak rays of the sun started streaking the sky. Dawn had come, and there would be much to do today. The two sisters' relationship had entered a new level of understanding. Their bond was stronger than ever. But they had other things to think of now. It would be Mishbee's job to help her sister dress for the wedding.

Soon the village was alive with morning activity. Mishbee's mother had moulded and dyed several clay beads that Oobata planned to wear in her hair. The sisters' father had caught an otter and had given Oobata the fur-laced skin to trim her brand-new mantle of caribou hide. Carefully, Mishbee helped Oobata put on her new mantle and leggings.

As Oobata reached for her broken comb to straighten her hair, her mother stopped her. "This comb isn't good anymore, Oobata. Today you're to be married. I have something I want you to have. Here, take this." She put her own beautiful comb made of bone in Oobata's hand. It was a present to her daughter, signifying that she had grown up.

A grateful tear escaped from one of Oobata's eyes. "Thank you, Mother," she almost sobbed.

Oobata fondled the exquisite comb. An intricately carved pattern decorated the top, and the teeth were in perfect condition. Oobata's grandfather had carved this comb for her mother many years ago. Oobata couldn't count the times she had longed to own such a beautiful comb herself. And now her mother was giving it to her. Accepting this gift of sacrifice, Oobata began the task of combing through her long dark hair. When it was as smooth as silk, Mishbee's mother plaited the hair, weaving the colourful clay beads between the shiny reams of hair. The effect was breathtaking. The dark, decorated mane was accentuated by the speckled colours of the beads. Mishbee looked at her sister with pride. Oobata was beautiful.

Together Oobata and Dematith stood before Chief Statuon. "I give you my blessing." He smeared red ochre on their foreheads, protecting their union from bad spirits. With that the entire village began feasting and singing. It was a long time since there had been a wedding, and everyone enjoyed the chance to celebrate all day and night. Mishbee memorized every face and every moment, for she wanted to etch it all permanently in her mind.

The days after the wedding were an adjustment for Mishbee. Sometimes she missed having Oobata beside her all the time. But Oobata seemed happy as Dematith's new wife, and Mishbee and Oobata still spent time together preparing and cooking fresh ptarmigan or lynx that the men brought back from their hunting. The sisters spoke very little of their secret, though it silently drew them even closer.

CHAPTER 8

John was deep in sleep. He dreamed he was back in England with his family, that it was springtime, and that it was unusually warm. It was Ruth's wedding day, and she was asking him how she looked in her wedding dress. Her hair was lighter than John's, almost golden, in fact. Ruth had very fair skin and delicate features and was quite slender. She was quite stately and proper in her gown. "John, John, John ..." she kept saying over and over. He was trying to answer her, but he couldn't seem to speak. She just kept calling his name over and over. *"John, John ..."*

Then he realized the voice belonged to Elizabeth Manuel, not his sister. Slowly, he shook himself awake and glanced at his bedroom door, immediately aware that he was still in Newfoundland, that it was terribly cold, and that winter wasn't over yet.

"John, it's time to get up," Mrs. Manuel said a little louder. "Answer me, boy."

"I'm awake, I'm awake," he finally mumbled.

John was warm beneath the heavy covers, but the air outside the blankets was frigid. He could see his breath and noticed a thin layer of frost on the window. The only thing John hated more than getting up on a cold winter day was going to bed on an equally chilly night. He dreaded the moment every winter evening when he had to leave the cozy fire of the kitchen to crawl into his ice-cold bed. Often he heated rocks in the fire ahead of time, then wrapped them in blankets and placed them between his covers to take away the frosty bite. There were many nights when his whole body shivered and his teeth chattered until his blankets finally warmed him up.

This morning, like every morning, there was no avoiding it. Even though it was still dark, it was time to get up. There was lots of work to do at the shipyard, and John knew he had to get moving. He counted to three in his head, then leaped out into the freezing air. Swiftly, he pulled on his clothes, which were as clammy as the room they had lain in all night.

Joseph was already up and eating breakfast when John sat down to sip his warm tea. The cup felt pleasant in his chilled hands, so he took a moment to envelop it with both palms, then sighed loudly.

"My, that was a heavy sigh, John," Joseph said. "What's on your mind?"

"The cold, I guess."

"Yes, 'tis part of this land. Not like old England, that's for sure. Well, there's work to be done. Eat up."

John nodded and quickly ate his biscuits, salted cod, and cheese.

Although she still busied herself and tended to chores around the house, Elizabeth moved a lot slower lately. The baby was due any day now. Sitting in a chair and resting, she said, "Don't work too hard now, men."

Joseph chuckled as he and John left the house. "We'll try."

Outside, it had snowed the night before and the island was covered in a pristine blanket of white. Even the craggy rocks on the hills and shoreline were dusted with snow, giving them a much softer, gentler appearance. Each step they took towards the shipyard was echoed with a crisp, squeaky reply in the winter air.

"It's beautiful after a snowfall, isn't it?" Joseph said.

John looked around. "Yes, it is." Then he shivered.

When they arrived at the shipyard, John went straight to the steam box, which was about five feet high and eighteen feet long. He collected scrap pieces of wood and immediately started the fire. Later that morning he would push planks of spruce, juniper, pine, and birch into the box so they could be made pliable by steaming and bending them into the desired curves. It was a difficult job and required a certain amount of skill, but John had become quite good at it.

As soon as the fire was going, Joseph came over and said, "John, there are a few things I'd like to show you."

John joined Joseph at the almost finished schooner, which had taken many men working hard all winter to build.

"You see these pieces here?" Joseph said, indicating the lower planks on the vessel as he ran his hands over the smooth wood. "What kind of wood is that?"

"I believe it's birch, isn't it?"

"It is. Any idea why we use birch?"

"Well, it's more durable." John looked up at the planking on the deck. "I guess you want a wood that lasts long under the waterline."

"Right you are. Save the birch for the water where durable matters the most." Joseph winked. "These kinds of answers are why your father sent you over here."

The two strolled over to the bow of the boat, which towered above them. "What are you going to name the ship, Joseph?"

"Funny thing really. I don't know. A shipbuilder never names his vessel before he builds it. But usually by this stage I have an idea what it should be called. Strangely, I have no ideas this time."

At that moment young Annie came running up, wide-eyed and completely out of breath.

"What are you doing in the shipyard, young lady?" Joseph asked. "And do your coat up. You'll catch your death of cold."

She ignored him. "Mr. Manuel, Mr. Manuel, you've got to come quick. Gertie sent me. Your missus ... she's having the baby. You better get home right away or you'll have Gertie to deal with instead of me."

"Today? She's ... she's having the baby today?" Joseph sputtered in disbelief.

True to form, Annie answered, "Yes, today, Mr. Manuel. Babies don't wait for the workday to be over to be born, you know. You better get home soon."

Annie turned around and headed back towards the house. Joseph followed behind bringing John reluctantly along. When they were nearly home, they heard the sounds of birthing. Joseph and John sat on the porch while Annie came out with updates every few minutes.

"Won't be much longer now, Mr. Manuel. Gertie says she can see the head." Moments later Annie reported back, "Shouldn't be too much longer, Mr. Manuel. Gertie says she can still see the head." After a little more time, Annie showed up once more. "Mr. Manuel, Gertie says the baby is well on its way. She says Mrs. Manuel is lucky to be moving along so quickly. Gertie says she's seen births that have taken sixteen hours, especially for the first one." Minutes later the cheeky little girl was out the front door again. "Gertie says it's a boy! She's just cleaning him up. She says you can come in now."

Joseph heaved a great sigh of relief, obviously over-joyed to hear this news. Childbirth was seldom easy on Exploits Island. This winter alone three women had died giving birth.

After Joseph went into his bedroom, John heard him call out, "Come here, John! Come see the baby!"

John wasn't too sure he wanted to be there. Tentatively, he poked his head in the doorway.

"Come all the way in, boy," Joseph urged. "The hard work's over."

John approached the bed and glimpsed a tiny, red, wrinkly little body wrapped tightly in clean blankets.

"You're looking at the next great schooner builder," Joseph said. "After you, of course."

"He's so small," John said in awe. "What are you go-ing to call him?"

"We've decided he'll be named Joseph after his fa-ther," Elizabeth said.

"It's funny," Joseph said. "I can't name that ship I have out at the yard, but naming a child was no problem at all. Some things just can't be explained."

John smiled, then excused himself to let the new family have some time alone. He figured he shouldn't go back to the shipyard without Joseph, so he got out his carving. The miniature schooner was starting to take shape. Relaxing into a chair beside the fireplace, he be-

gan to carve. Before he knew it the wood and the daylight hours were whittled away.

That evening Joseph placed his new son in John's
arms. "Here, hold him."

John gazed in wonder at the button eyes sealed shut
and marvelled at the tiny fingers in the clenched fists.
It was hard to imagine this little baby growing up to be
a full-grown man. Seeing and holding the infant made
John homesick and reminded him that he was far removed from his own sister and father. His sister, Ruth,
had been like a mother to John. She had always believed
in him and his grand schemes. When others had told
John that he was only a boy and patronized his ideas of
going to the New World, Ruth had listened to and en-
couraged his dreams of seeking out a new life and want-
ing to become a carpenter.

Handing little Joseph back to his father, John went
to his bedroom and stared out his window at the ocean.
Sighing, he went to his dresser and pulled out his father's
pocket watch. This was his one connection to his past.
He stood there for a long time in thought. Finally, he put
the watch down and wrote a letter by candlelight:

Dearest Ruth,

I imagine your anticipation at your
approaching wedding grows greater with
every day. I wish I had been there in person to congratulate you when you announced your engagement. I want you to
know again, as I wrote earlier, that I am
very happy for you and George.

Things are going well here. It has been a long and sometimes tiresome winter, much rougher than the weather at home. The house here can get very cold at night. The Manuels' bedroom is close to the fireplace, but my room is at the far end of the house and can be bitterly cold at night. The blankets are often like sheets of ice.

The schooner is almost finished. I'm pleased to say that I think I've been a help to Mr. Manuel. He doesn't hesitate to tell me how well I'm doing. However, Mr. Manuel doesn't know what to call the ship yet.

Today was very eventful as Mrs. Manuel had a baby. The mother and tiny boy, who they have named Joseph after his father, are healthy and happy. Mr. Manuel let me hold the baby tonight. It is hard to believe that you and I were ever that small.

I am very lonely as my friend Allen is winterhousing (as they call it here) on the main island. Winterhousing is when the men go inland and hunt, trap, or cut wood. They live in a makeshift building that they put together quickly themselves. Allen has established a trapping line where he snares animals for meat and furs. I'm looking forward to his return, which should be in the very near future.

Give my regards to Father.

Sincerely,
John

He folded the letter, blew out the candle, and forced himself to crawl under the covers. Due to all the excitement of the day, he had forgotten to warm a rock to put in his bed ahead of time. He shook and chattered in the chilly blankets.

The next few days were quite an adjustment for the Manuel family. Sleep was often interrupted by the cries of a hungry baby, and it seemed as if Gertie was always at the house helping with the washing, the baking, and the cleaning or tending to the baby to give Elizabeth a break. Joseph continued to go out to the shipyard to make sure that everyone was working to the plan. Being the master builder brought a lot of responsibility with it, but he often headed out a little later and went home a little earlier.

One evening, after John had helped Elizabeth with baby Joseph, a surprise visitor arrived at the house.

"Well, look at this, would you?" Joseph said. "If it isn't Allen."

Allen was scruffier and looked a little weathered.

"You're back!" John cried, instantly thinking of Mishbee. "How was your time in the tilt? Anything eventful happen?" he asked with some trepidation.

Allen laughed. "Nothing a musket couldn't take care of."

John's alarm increased. "Did you meet anything or *anyone* unexpectedly?"

"No, nothing really. Of course, there was the usual wildlife on the trapping line. We didn't even run into a bear this year. I'm glad to be back, though."

"I imagine you are," Elizabeth interjected. "Back where you can get a decent washing up and some good food. Here, sit and I'll pour you some tea."

Allen pulled up a chair and sat down. "Thank you, Mrs. Manuel. That would be most welcome. I hear congratulations are in order. I'm told you've had a baby boy."

"Indeed we have. I'd show little Joseph to you, but he's asleep." Elizabeth smiled. "So have you seen Miss Wells yet?"

Allen blushed a little. It was no secret that he had his heart set on that young lady. "Not yet. I just came back today and haven't had a chance to clean up properly. Maybe tomorrow I'll call on her."

"Good enough," Elizabeth said as she handed Allen a cup of tea.

Allen looked squarely at John. "How's the schooner coming along?"

"It's almost done. You'll have to come to the shipyard tomorrow and see for yourself."

"I'll do that." Allen turned to Joseph. "Have you named the ship?"

"Not yet," Joseph said. "That will have to come soon, though. I'm hoping young John has some ideas. I thought maybe we could name her together."

"What would you like to call the ship, John?" Allen asked.

"I don't know. I haven't given it much thought, since I expected Mr. Manuel to name it."

Allen smiled at his friend. "It looks like you better start thinking."

They visited until everyone was so tired they could barely keep their eyes open. After an extra-long yawn, Allen announced, "I better go home so you good folks can get some sleep. I'll be by the shipyard tomorrow, John, to see your work. It better be up to my standards."

John grinned. "Oh, it is. You'll see."

The next day Allen was at the shipyard bright and early. "I'm impressed," he told John and Joseph, marvelling at the schooner. He picked up an auger. "Can I help?"

"Certainly," Joseph said. "Make yourself useful and help me drill some holes for these nails.

Allen enjoyed his time at the shipyard and came by often to lend a hand. John liked having someone at the yard closer to his age, and he and Allen often chatted while they worked. Their conversations usually revolved around Exploits, ships, England, trapping, and hunting, but never about the people of the red ochre. John didn't want to revive painful memories for Allen of his dead brother. There were times when John wanted to share his precious secret about Mishbee with someone … anyone. But Allen could never be that person.

Sometimes it seemed impossible to keep the knowledge of Mishbee to himself. There were moments when John thought about telling Elizabeth Manuel or Annie, or even writing his sister about the Red Indian girl. But he knew his secret would only alarm them, especially his sister who was so far away.

One night, when John and Allen were walking home, John noticed the snow melting off the evergreens. The hypnotic *drip-drip* of water falling steadily onto the path caught his ears. He glanced around. Everywhere the snow was vanishing. It was getting warmer. Winter was loosening its grip and spring would soon arrive. It wouldn't be long before Mishbee's people would return to the coast and John could go back to the pond and maybe, just maybe, find his secret friend one more time.

CHAPTER 9

Winter had turned into an early spring and now it was time for yet another celebration — the Red Ochre Festival. Mishbee's tribe gathered at a place the settlers called Red Indian Lake. Next to the caribou run, this was the biggest celebration of the year. It was a time when everyone received a new ceremonial application of red ochre and infants were initiated with their first coat of the sacred mixture.

This year there was only one new child in the entire group. She was a girl born just before autumn arrived. The chief stood tall and commanded, "Bring me Shanawdithit."

The baby was brought before the chief. Carefully, he applied the greasy substance over the tiny, wiggly girl. The tribe sang in celebration as he did this.

"Today this girl brings us hope," the chief told his people. "She represents the hope of our people, the hope of our way of life, the hope of our tradition, and the hope of our future. We are few in this land and we have many enemies. The Micmac and the settlers take from us. But we must survive. Our children must survive. This infant is important. She is one of us, still young and a symbol of our future. Today we honour her and set her before the

Great Spirit." The chief held the baby high in triumph, and the celebrations began.

After the festivities, Mishbee was restless. She walked listlessly around the camp, feeling a little lost until she heard Dematith's familiar voice.

"Come, Little Bird, watch this," he beckoned. "I wish to entice your father into a game. Do you think it can be done?"

Mishbee knew her father loved to take on any challenge. She smiled at Dematith. "I think you'll be successful."

They walked over to where her father sat. "I challenge you to a game," Dematith said to him.

Both Mishbee and Oobata listened attentively to the ensuing conversation.

Their father thought for a moment, then said, "I take you up on this challenge."

The two men sat on the ground, and several other people joined Mishbee and Oobata to watch. Between the two men lay several carved dice in a bowl. Mishbee's father threw the dice from the bowl first.

"Ah, Dematith, my score is three."

Dematith didn't seem alarmed. Everyone looked on as he took a turn throwing the dice. "But see, my score is five."

Mishbee's father shrugged. His next throw was six.

The game continued, with Dematith sometimes ahead and Mishbee's father sometimes in the lead. It was entertaining to watch the men take this mock competition so seriously.

Mishbee glanced around and saw that many other groups of people were playing bowl games. Others were carving and some were singing. The whole village was a celebration of life. Another year had passed and the future looked bright indeed.

With the return of spring the smaller hunting bands once again dispersed to the coastal regions to hunt. Mishbee's group ended up not far from where it had been the previous year, and each day the memory of John became stronger and stronger for Mishbee. She often found herself thinking about where he lived, what his people did to survive, where he was now. Coming back to the same area where she had first met the stranger made her even more curious about him. Mishbee wondered if she would ever see John again.

Such thoughts made her uncomfortable. These days she often avoided Oobata, fearing her sister could read her mind. One morning Mishbee sneaked off towards the pond where she had first come across John. She waited there as long as she could afford to, knowing her absence would be noticed if she didn't return soon. But no settler came there that day, so she went back to the camp in disappointment.

The memory of John couldn't be erased, though. She was compelled to go back to the pond each morning for almost a week, but John still didn't turn up.

"Where are you?" she would say to no one in particular. "Do your people have feasts and celebrations as we do? Do you hunt for caribou and sing at weddings? Why don't you cover yourself with red ochre? I want to learn more about your people. Please come back."

The only creatures that heard Mishbee's questions were the fish in the pond and the birds in the nearby trees. Day after day no one answered her. Finally, Mishbee decided that John would never return. The Good Spirit had only sent him once and that was all. She gave up her search.

The next morning the men in her band went out to gather great auk eggs. The harvest was good that day, and Mishbee and Oobata were given a great deal to do. Oobata lifted the boiled eggs from the birchbark pot and placed them on a flat rock where they would be dried and later pounded into fine powder to mix with other food.

"Do you see my stomach?" Oobata asked as she worked.

"Yes," Mishbee said, not paying much attention to her sister. She was preparing finely cut bits of seal fat to mix with the eggs. This, too, would be dried in the sun. If the men were successful spearing another harp seal in the bay, she would also make a type of sausage consisting of seal flesh, fat, liver, and eggs.

"Mishbee, you're not paying attention," Oobata chided.

A little annoyed, Mishbee glanced up. "What is it?"

Oobata took Mishbee's hand and rubbed it over her stomach. Mishbee felt a tiny bulge as her hand slid over her sister's belly. "You're with child!" she cried.

Oobata smiled. "Yes, I am!"

"That's wonderful. I'm so happy for you. I'll be an aunt!"

After they finished with the eggs, Mishbee decided to take a walk down the coast to collect periwinkle snails. The tiny snails lined the shore, and Mishbee busied herself harvesting them. She was always aware of her surroundings, and long before she was spotted she detected a boat on the horizon headed towards the shore. It wasn't a canoe, but a settlers' vessel. Quickly, Mishbee hid behind some trees at the top of a cliff where she could watch but not be seen. The boat came closer, and her sharp eyes spotted two boys in it. One of them was her settler friend!

John was saying something to his companion. Even though it had been many months since she had heard him talk, his voice sounded friendly and very familiar to her. She studied him at a distance. He seemed sturdier and his shoulders were broader, but he looked more weathered after a long winter.

The two boys secured their boat, jumped ashore, and discussed something. John pointed in the direction of the pond. The other boy, who looked older than John, had a harsher voice. Mishbee didn't like the way he spoke. The other boy pointed his musket down the coast. John shook his head.

The two trudged up the hill towards the pond. Mishbee was intrigued. She knew it was dangerous, and Oobata wouldn't approve, but she followed, anyway. When the two arrived at the pond, John sat on the rock where he had placed Mishbee's berries and the repaired pendant the previous summer. The harsh boy said something and shook his head. John said something back, then the harsh boy shook his head again and stomped noisily into the woods towards the coast. Remaining behind, John sighed and stared at the pond.

Mishbee watched for a while. She didn't want to put herself in danger. She found a small stone and threw it into a brook, causing John to turn his head in the other direction. "Mishbee?" he called out.

He was looking for her! She threw another stone.

"Is that you, Mishbee?"

She felt safe. John's presence wasn't a trap. Gaining courage, and ignoring the warnings of her people, she stepped out of hiding into John's view.

"Mishbee," he repeated, this time more quietly.

She nodded. "John ..." He seemed pleased that she had remembered his name.

"I was hoping you'd be here again. I wondered about you all winter. I worried how you could survive in the cold weather in the bush. I barely survived in the Manuels' house! This land has terrible winters."

Mishbee didn't understand a word John said, but if she had, she would have told him she also had wondered about him.

For a moment John said nothing. He seemed lost in thought, then looked at Mishbee and smiled. "Oh, this is for you." He reached into his pocket, pulled out a carving strung on a thin piece of leather, and held it out to her.

Mishbee blinked, uncertain what to do.

"It's for you, Mishbee," he told her. "Take it."

She didn't move.

"It's a pendant."

When Mishbee remained motionless, John took the pendant and placed it over her head. She peered at the strange carving. It wasn't made of bone or antler. Instead, it was fashioned from wood, which didn't make sense to her. A pendant of wood would deteriorate over time. The design on the object wasn't a shape or an animal but a carving that looked a lot like a settlers' ship.

"It's a schooner," John said. "I'm an apprentice and I'm learning how to build these ships from Mr. Manuel.

There were a lot of winter nights when there wasn't much else to do except carve. I know how much you like pendants. Mrs. Manuel kept asking, 'What are you up to, young John?' And I would answer, 'Just carving.' That never seemed to satisfy her curiosity, though. She simply couldn't understand why I would waste my time on such foolishness. If she only knew the real reason I was carving, she'd be completely beside herself."

Mishbee nodded at his chatter and accepted the unusual gift. She hadn't brought anything for John. She glanced around to see what she could give him, then went over and stripped some birchbark from a nearby tree. *"Paushee,"* she said, pointing at the bark.

"Paushee," John repeated.

Mishbee tore more bark off the tree and handed it to John. Then she motioned for him to sit on the rock with her. Her nimble fingers folded the bark, and she indicated that John should mimic her actions. Awkwardly, he tried to follow her directions, but it was no use. She giggled at his attempts and took the bark back from him, using it to create a tiny yet sturdy basket. John was impressed with the speed and ease with which she did this. When she was finished, she put it in his hands.

"For me?" John asked. "I couldn't take this ..." He shook his head and gave the basket back to Mishbee, which caused her to frown.

She couldn't understand why he wouldn't accept her gift. The settlers were hard to figure out. Nevertheless, Mishbee smiled and led him over the hill and back to the shoreline. She put her small pile of snails into the basket and began gathering more.

"You eat these?" John asked. "Of course, you aren't going to answer me." He laughed and helped her collect the little creatures.

They worked and walked, though they didn't speak much. When Mishbee had enough snails, they headed back to the pond.

"What else do you eat?" John asked. "Do you eat turnips, or cabbage, or salt fish?"

Mishbee smiled, wishing she could understand his speech. Then, suddenly out of nowhere, an arm reached out of the brush, grabbed Mishbee violently, and pulled her behind a tree in one fluid motion. John recoiled in astonishment. Mishbee would have screamed except another hand flew around and planted itself firmly across her mouth. It felt as if her heart were beating in her throat.

Totally caught off guard, John simply stared in complete disbelief. Behind the tree was a girl who had similar features to Mishbee's but who looked a little older. The strange girl's hair was long and plaited with colourful beads. Her eyes pierced John's with intense fierceness as she motioned with her head for him to keep walking with an urgency he dared not question. Then John heard a snap a little farther ahead in the thick alders.

He did his best to think clearly. What could that noise be? *Allen!* Wasting no time, he called out, "Allen!"

"Blast it, John! Is that you? I thought I had a hare. I was sure something was behind that tree over there just behind you."

John picked up his pace immediately, forcing himself

not to bolt into a full-fledged run. He realized the second Red Indian girl had been aware of Allen's presence and had probably saved Mishbee's life.

"I'm sure it was just your imagination, Allen," John said, standing beside his friend now.

"No, I really think there's a hare behind that tree. Stand still. I'm going to take a shot."

John's mind raced. Allen had his musket up and ready to shoot. Mishbee was in the line of fire! He had to react immediately or it would be too late.

"No!" John yelled, pushing Allen's gun aside as the shot rang out.

"Have you gone stark raving mad?" Allen demanded. "That was possibly my supper you scared away. What on earth has gotten into you?"

"I ... I know there was nothing back there. I just came from there. I didn't want you to waste your shot."

"Waste my shot! And screaming and pushing my gun around is saving my shot? Honestly, John, stick to building schooners."

Mishbee could have reached out and touched the harsh boy as he and John passed by on the way to their boat, but he didn't see her or Oobata, for the two sisters were so still they hardly breathed. When the young men were safely out on the ocean, Mishbee and Oobata dared to move.

"I owe you my life, Oobata. How did you know?"

"I've been watching you, Mishbee. I followed you every day you went to the pond the last while. I watch you in the camp. I see when you leave."

Mishbee bowed her head in shame. "I should have been more careful."

"Mishbee, you *must* listen to me. Your friend John is of the Good Spirit, as you say, but his friend is not. If I hadn't been here, you would have been killed. You can't keep doing this. It will only bring destruction." Oobata noticed the odd pendant around Mishbee's neck. "What's that?"

"John gave it to me. It's a pendant of a settlers' ship."

"It's not like anything Dematith makes. It's different. It's made of wood."

"Yes, it isn't like anything I've seen before, either."

"What will you do with this gift?" Oobata asked as she felt the smoothness of the carved wood.

"It comes from the Good Spirit to protect me. I must keep it."

"You can't tell Mother that you got it from a settler!"

"No, you're right. I can never do that." Mishbee stood silently, not knowing what to do or say.

"Put it on the ground," Oobata said.

"What? I have to keep this!" Mishbee protested. She didn't want to give up her new gift.

"Put it on the ground," Oobata ordered, this time more authoritatively.

"Oobata, you know I want to … I must keep this."

"You'll keep it, Mishbee. Believe in me. I'm your sister. Put it on the ground."

Doubtfully, Mishbee placed the pendant on the ground.

Oobata scooped up the pendant. "Ah, look at what I found lying in the woods, Mishbee. I'm going to take it back to camp to show everyone what I found and then

I'm going to give it to my sister."

Mishbee was pleased with Oobata's plan.

"Mishbee, more and more of our people are bringing home things the settlers leave behind. It won't be questioned if *I* bring this back. *You*, on the other hand, with your unexplained absences might have a problem."

"You're right, Oobata. Thank you."

Then, without another word but with yet another secret, the two sisters walked back to their summer encampment.

John arrived back on Exploits Island tired and preoccupied with the memory of what had happened that afternoon. As soon as he entered the Manuels' house, he went to his room and discovered a letter from his sister lying on his bed. Eagerly, he opened the letter and read its contents:

Dearest John,

> We truly miss you. I trust everything is going well in that rugged land you now call home.
>
> I know that you couldn't return for the wedding. However, you were missed. It was a beautiful winter day, and Aunt Beatrice and Uncle Ivan came all the way from London for the ceremony. Uncle Ivan is very interested in what you're doing in Newfoundland. He says he had a mind to do the same a few years back.

Father is well, and the old house is holding up reasonably. George and I have settled a few miles away in Mrs. Elerby's old cottage. It suits us well.

As for naming the ship, I think you should call it something meaningful. Pick whatever is dearest to your heart and that should be its name!

With much love,
Ruth

CHAPTER 10

Early one morning, Dissik, a man from another hunting group, came running into Mishbee's camp. It was uncharacteristic for him to be at their summer camp. Alarmed at his unexpected presence, Mishbee's band gathered around him.

"Why are you here?" Dematith asked.

"I'm a messenger with terrible news. Chief Statuon is dead! He was out hunting in the woods and happened upon some white men. It was a small group, but his arrows were no match for what he met. He was killed by the powerful thunder of the white trappers."

Mishbee went numb and averted Oobata's chilling glare. Then her sister leaned closer and whispered, "This is a warning, Mishbee."

It was decided at once that the band would travel inland to the chief's summer residence. They didn't talk or sing during their canoe journey. Each member of Mishbee's band was filled with memories and sadness. In a short time the tribe would commit their chief to the New Land.

It was strange to see almost the entire tribe again before autumn, but the reunion didn't give Mishbee the usual pleasure. Several people busied themselves preparing for the coming ceremony. Solemnly, red ochre was spread over the chief's body, which was then wrapped in birchbark. Next, his prized possessions were collected. The spirits of these belongings would follow the chief's soul into the afterlife. After the chief's things were assembled, they and his body were put into a canoe.

Mishbee studied the limp, lifeless package that lay in the vessel and replayed the images of her sister's wedding in her mind. She recalled how Chief Statuon had stood before Dematith and Oobata, valued sceptre in hand, to give his blessing to the couple. Now it was his turn to be in need of blessing.

It was time to commit the chief's soul to the afterlife. The members of the tribe got into their canoes and paddled out to a small nearby island. Mishbee sat close to Oobata but still avoided her gaze. When they reached the island, some of the stronger men of the tribe gently carried the chief's body to an isolated cave carved into a cliff that opened out onto the Great Lake. Close by, the tribe chanted the burial song with deep respect as elders placed the chief's treasures around him in the cave.

At the next sunrise Chief Statuon's spirit would travel to the New Land. Mishbee wished him well in his journey as she crawled back into the wide centre of a canoe for the voyage back to the mainland. She would miss the great leader.

As soon as Mishbee and her sister returned to the chief's summer camp, Oobata finally had her say. "See what these settlers can do? They kill even our leader!"

"Oobata, you heard Dissik. It wasn't a settler. It was a trapper. It wasn't John or even his harsh friend. I mourn for the loss of Chief Statuon. I've even allowed myself to dream of the day when he would stand before me at *my* wedding and grant me his blessing. I've even imagined him blessing your newborn baby one day. I'm shocked and I'm upset with his senseless death." She touched the schooner pendant hanging around her neck. "But John didn't kill our beloved chief."

"Mishbee, I know John didn't, but his people are still dangerous. Coming too close to the settlers is deadly. You must keep your distance. I worry so much about you, Little Bird. You're too trusting."

Despite her sister's concern, Mishbee was compelled to make regular visits to the pond after her band returned to its coastal camp. She hoped very much to see John one more time before the next winter. Mishbee never spotted Oobata on these trips, but she wondered if her sister was still keeping an eye on her. She took comfort in this thought, though she never asked Oobata to confirm her suspicion.

About a week later Mishbee caught sight of John at the pond. She didn't see any sign of his harsh friend but was cautious, anyway, as she glided quietly out into the open.

"Mishbee, you're here!" John cried, whirling around. "I thought you'd never return after that near miss with Allen's musket. I wouldn't blame you in the least. You're very fortunate. That boy thought he had a hare, you know. He hasn't forgiven me for ruining his aim. As you can see, I didn't bring him today. I came alone for your well-being as well as mine."

John pointed to himself, then held up his forefinger, indicating he was only one person. He repeated this gesture several times, motioned towards the woods where the harsh boy had gone the last time, and said, "Allen isn't here."

Mishbee smiled when she finally understood that the harsh boy wasn't with him.

"I brought you something," John said. "Here, keep this."

It was a piece of salt cod. Mishbee took the gift and nodded acceptance. She sat beside John and deftly opened a small folded piece of birchbark, revealing a portion of the red ochre powder that glistened on her skin. "*Odeman,*" she said.

"*Odeman,*" John repeated.

Mishbee wanted to tell John that this sacred mixture would keep away evil spirits and protect his fair skin from the sun and insects, but she knew he wouldn't understand her words. Instead, she took his arm and rubbed some of the powder on the back of his hand.

"Thank you," he said. "So it's called *odeman*, is it? We call it red ochre." He looked at Mishbee and pointed to his hand. "Red ochre," he said.

She smiled. "Red ochre."

"That's right. Very good." He pointed at her leather shoes. "What are those called?"

Mishbee glanced at her feet. "*Moosin.*"

"Interesting."

Mishbee reached out to touch John's hair. He backed away at first, but then let her feel his hair. She had never seen hair this colour before meeting John. "*Drona,*" she said, touching his hair, then her own.

"*Drona,*" he echoed.

Mishbee walked towards the pond and scooped

some water out, letting it trickle between her fingers. *"Ebanthoo."*

John grinned. "Let's see. *Ebanthoo* — water. Well, my hope is to catch some trout out of this *ebanthoo* today. Do you fish?" He showed her a long stick. "This is my fishing rod."

Mishbee didn't understand what the instrument was for. Quietly, she sat and watched as he put a worm on a hook and cast the line out into the pond. It didn't take long for him to catch a fish, and Mishbee was fascinated by this new way of getting trout from the pond.

Out of the corner of her eye, Mishbee detected a slight movement. It was no more noticeable than a leaf wrinkling in a breeze, but Mishbee detected it. Oobata was watching in the nearby alders.

"Who was that girl who pulled you behind the tree during my last and somewhat eventful visit?" John asked.

Mishbee had no idea what he was talking about now but continued to watch as he cast his line back into the water.

"She looked a lot like you, only a little taller and maybe a little older. I wonder if that was your sister. I have a sister named Ruth. So perhaps we have that in common, too. My sister means a lot to me. After my mother died, she took care of me. It seems like your sister does the same for you. She certainly protected you from Allen."

When Mishbee failed to say anything, John continued to chatter. "I miss England, but things are good here, too. I'm getting more and more skilled at building schooners. Mr. Manuel let me do quite a bit of work on the ship we've almost finished. I love working with wood.

Mr. Manuel says my work is impeccable and that I love detail. I really enjoy creating a ship, and I think I'm good at it. I believe each schooner takes on a living personality of its own. We still have to name the one we're nearly finished. Ruth says I should name it after something dear to my heart."

Mishbee suddenly stood and started to walk away.

"Are you leaving now?" John asked, alarm in his voice. Don't! Please stop!"

Mishbee halted and turned to look at him.

"When will I see you again?" John asked. "Next time I'll bring something to write on so I can learn more of your language and you can learn more of mine. Let's meet again the day after tomorrow."

Mishbee stared blankly. She could see that he, like her, was frustrated at their inability to communicate.

Suddenly, John grabbed some twigs and put one on the ground. "Today," he said, pointing at the sun. He put another twig on the ground. "Tomorrow." Then he put a third stick beside the first two. "The next day. We'll meet here." He indicated the pond.

Mishbee smiled and nodded. She understood the sticks. She would return the day after tomorrow. Then, without another word or gesture, Mishbee disappeared into the brush where Oobata was now waiting.

"See, he isn't of the Bad Spirit," she told her sister.

"I see …" Oobata said thoughtfully. "Mishbee, how many more times are you going to visit him? You can't keep coming here. Just what are you trying to do?"

"I'm not trying to do anything. I'm curious, and so are you. Why else did you come out to watch him from the alders?"

"I came to watch over you, Mishbee."

"You wanted to see the stranger, too! You're as curious as I am."

"How dare you accuse me of such things, especially after I saved your life!" Oobata said.

Mishbee sighed. "Oh, Oobata, I'm sorry. I'm not trying to make you angry."

"It's forbidden. Good Spirit or Bad Spirit, it's forbidden. Why must you keep me in your web of secrecy and worry?"

Mishbee had never given much thought before about how this secret must weigh upon Oobata. It hadn't occurred to her that this illicit secret would cause Oobata such anguish. "I'm sorry, Oobata. I'm so sorry."

"It's just that so much evil has happened, Mishbee. The chief has been killed, and it seems that every year there are fewer and fewer of us. I know how much Mother and Father would disapprove of what you're doing, and I carry all this heavy knowledge inside me. I don't want you to be hurt, Little Bird. I would feel responsible if you were."

"I don't mean to cause you pain with this secret, Oobata. You know that, don't you?"

"I do, but sometimes my heart feels as if it will burst. You mean so much to me, Mishbee!"

"I'll be more careful, Oobata. I give you my word."

"It's not your word I'm concerned about, Little Bird, but the thunder of the settlers' weapons."

CHAPTER 11

There was a lightness in John's step as he hiked back to his boat after the meeting with Mishbee. Although the return trip to Exploits Island would be lengthy, he didn't care, for he was excited about seeing Mishbee again in two days. He would bring his journal this time and write down the new words he learned. Travelling this distance alone in a boat was dangerous on the always unpredictable sea, but he was willing to chance it.

When John arrived back at Exploits, he knew he would be interrogated about his lengthy absence by one or both of the Manuels. No sooner had he shut the door to their house than he heard Elizabeth ask, "John, is that you, boy?"

"Yes, Mrs. Manuel, it's me."

"I'm glad you're back. Just a minute while I put the baby down." A few moments later Elizabeth came into the kitchen, a stern expression on her face. "Where were you today, John?"

Despite knowing he would likely face such a question, he was still caught off guard and stalled by not answering right away.

"Honestly, I don't know another young man who daydreams as much you do!"

John pulled himself together finally. "I went for a trip and brought back some trout, Mrs. Manuel." He held up his catch for her to inspect.

She scrutinized the fish, then noticed his hands. "My goodness, what's all that red dirt?"

John blushed. He had forgotten about the red ochre. "I must have gotten dirty fishing at the pond."

"I can't say I understand all of this trip-taking, John. You and I both know that the best schooners in the world are built right here on this little island of ours, and if you're planning on becoming a force in Joseph's business, you're going to have to settle yourself right where you are. I can't imagine what you're doing with all this gallivanting around! I have a mind to write your father and tell him all the nonsense you're up to."

No matter what John told Elizabeth, she would still view his trips to the main island as downright foolishness, and telling her the truth would only alarm her even more. So he said nothing.

"Do you need something to eat, John?" she finally asked. "Joseph is visiting friends and won't be home until late tonight."

"Yes, some food would be good, thank you." John felt hunger pangs assailing his stomach. A good supper was just what he needed.

As John sat down to a meal of cod and cabbage, he thought about his day. It already seemed like an eternity since he had last talked with Mishbee. As far as he was concerned, two days couldn't pass quickly enough. He felt a slight pain nagging his chest and figured he had been exposed to too much wind on the boat ride back from the main island.

After supper, John went promptly to bed. The events of the day had exhausted him body and soul, and sleep quickly came as soon as he lay down. Although his mind frequently wandered during the daylight hours, no dreams haunted him that night.

The next morning John awakened in a fit of coughing. He felt a little warm and had a burning sensation in his chest. Maybe he was getting a touch of influenza. There were many things he had to do today, so he ignored the general queasiness he was experiencing.

"Good morning," Joseph greeted as John seated himself at the kitchen table. "Elizabeth says you were out travelling again yesterday."

"Yes, I caught some trout," John said, hoping Joseph wouldn't press for more specific details about his trip.

"Could you stop by the shipyard later today?" Joseph asked. "We still need to finish up some odds and ends on that schooner. And, of course, she needs a name."

"I'd love to go to the yard. I'm visiting Allen this morning and running a few errands, then I'll be right over."

"Excellent."

As soon as he finished his breakfast, John went to call on Allen, who he hadn't seen for a while. He wondered if Allen was still upset about his behaviour when he spoiled his friend's aim. Entering Allen's house, he wasn't surprised to see a certain young woman sitting in the front room.

"Good day, Miss Wells," John said cordially. It was no secret that Allen was a possible suitor for Miss Wells. In fact, most people believed they would marry quite soon.

"Good day," she replied politely.

"Well, John, good to see you," Allen said, coming out of the kitchen.

"I'm a little surprised to hear you say that given your feelings about me the last time we were together."

"Yes, well, a hare is a good meal, you know. There are many things I don't understand about you, but you're still my friend." He slapped John heartily on the back, causing him to break into a coughing fit.

"Sorry there, John. I didn't think I hit you that hard."

"I must have something caught in my throat," John rasped. He turned to the young lady. "How is your mother, Miss Wells?"

"As good as can be expected. This land can be hard on a person."

John smiled ruefully. "That is certainly true."

"Have you seen my niece Annie lately, John?" Allen asked.

"No, as a matter of fact, it's been a few days. Usually, she comes to the shipyard regularly, but she must have been busy this week."

"I ran into her down at the general store a couple of days ago, and she was asking about you. For some reason beyond me she thinks the world of you. I was going to tell her you were out scaring rabbits, but I thought better of it."

John cleared his throat. "Well, thank you for that small mercy, Allen. I best be going, though. Joseph wants me at the shipyard. It was nice seeing you, Miss Wells."

She smiled. "You, too, John."

By coincidence, on the way to the shipyard, John spotted Annie skipping and singing merrily. She was always so full of energy, and today her chestnut-brown hair seemed to sparkle in the morning light.

"John, John," she squealed when she spied him, "I'm going to pick some raspberries for my family. Do you want to come?"

Her enthusiasm was too great to destroy. Joseph and the shipyard could wait a few more minutes. "I guess so, Annie. How have you been this past while?"

"Splendid!"

The two headed towards the other side of the path where raspberries grew profusely. Annie danced around the bushes, picking berries and talking at full speed. "You know, John, my sister, Sarah, says she saw a bear not far from our house last week. Do you believe it?" She didn't give John time to respond. "A bear! I think she's fibbing, but I'm not absolutely sure ..."

Annie continued to talk about bears, berries, and everything that had happened to her since John had last seen her. He listened attentively and kept picking raspberries. Just hearing Annie jabber made him incredibly tired. No one else could have that much energy. Soon Annie's container was full, and she told him she should head home.

"Now, Annie, you be a good help to your father," John instructed.

"I always am, John. See you later, and thanks for helping me with the berries."

Amused by the little girl's prattling, he watched her scamper down the path towards the settlement. "My pleasure, Annie," he called after her.

"John!" he heard another voice call from behind him. He turned to see the elder John Peyton walking up the pathway towards him.

"Good day, Mr. Peyton."

"Hello, John. Mr. Manuel tells me you were a big help building that beautiful schooner over in his shipyard. He says you're a good worker. Now tell me, what's a fine young man like yourself wasting your time building schooners when you could be fishing? I'm always looking for people to help me with the salmon fishing. I have a station up the Exploits River just itching for a few more good men."

"Thank you, Mr. Peyton, but I'm quite satisfied at the moment."

John Peyton winked. "Suit yourself. But if you ever get tired of the way Mr. Manuel treats you, come talk to me."

"I'll keep that in mind," John said as the man continued on his way. He knew full well he would never tire of the treatment he received from Joseph Manuel!

John strolled on towards the shipyard. When he arrived, he noticed Mr. Lily and Joseph deep in conversation.

"Hello," John said.

"Good morning, John," Mr. Lily boomed cheerily.

John was about to greet Joseph when once again he was overcome by uncontrollable, deeply painful coughs.

"What's wrong, John?" Mr. Lily asked. "You're sounding mighty sick there, boy. You don't have consumption, do you? If you do, you better go to bed right away. This community doesn't need another bout of that, you know."

"Consumption!" John said. "Don't be silly. It's just the morning air." Inwardly, though, he began to worry.

"You're certain you're all right, John?" Joseph asked, concern in his voice.

"I'm fine, Mr. Manuel. Really I am."

However, as John and Joseph went to work to complete the finishing touches on the schooner, John's coughing only increased.

"I'm worried about that cough of yours," Joseph finally said, eyeing his apprentice closely.

"I … I know," John said between coughs. Things were rapidly getting worse. He shouldn't have ignored the signs and symptoms.

"How long have you been like this, John?" Joseph asked. "You should have told me you weren't feeling well."

"I've been coughing a little for three or four days, but until today I thought I was just catching a cold or maybe a touch of flu."

Joseph frowned. "That's no cold or flu, John. We need to get you home."

John knew it was consumption. In the past year too many people on the island had died from the terrible disease. The dreaded consumption ate holes in your lungs, causing you to hemorrhage profusely. Some people survived this transplanted European plague and others simply did not. The only known remedies for the affliction were complete and utter bed rest to allow the lungs to heal and daily doses of cod liver oil.

Strangely enough, John found himself more worried about missing his next meeting with Mishbee. He so wanted to see her again to learn more about her people and language. But he knew that would be unlikely now. At the moment his coughing was so severe it was debilitating. The gripping pain penetrated his lungs with a depth he couldn't describe.

"We have to get you home now, John," Joseph said, his eyes indicating he would brook no argument. "Come on, boy, let's get you back to the house and into bed. You're in no shape to be up and about." He put his arm around his apprentice and steered him up the path towards home.

"Get the bed ready," Joseph told his wife as he entered the house.

Gertie was visiting.

"Take that baby back to your house, Gertie," Joseph said. "No one is to come visit for a while. It appears we have a sick lad to mind. Please hurry."

Elizabeth took one look at John and gasped, "Consumption!"

Joseph nodded gravely. He didn't have to say anything else. Consumption was no stranger to Elizabeth Manuel. She had lost many friends to the disease. Quickly, she readied John's bed for his arrival.

"Make it stop!" John cried out as she put him to bed. His lungs burned, sweat seemed to slide off him in waves, and he was more miserable than he had ever been.

"Shh, my boy, shh," Elizabeth whispered, trying to soothe him.

To John's horror he began to cough again. This time he expelled a trickle of red ooze from his mouth, which gushed farther and stronger with every cough. His lungs were bleeding. There was no doubt now that he was afflicted with consumption.

The coughing bout finally ceased, and he lay quietly, listening to his laboured breathing. Then another series of coughs wracked him, and he panicked. "Mother?" he cried.

"Your mother's gone, John," Elizabeth said, trying to calm the frightened boy. "But I'm here, my dear."

"Oh … yes, she's gone." He looked around him, his eyes wild. "Ruth, where's Ruth?"

"John, that's your fever talking. Ruth is back in England, along with your father. Save your strength now and get some rest."

That's right, he thought. *Mother has died, and Ruth and Father are in England. Yes, of course, I'm on Exploits Island. Tomorrow I'm going to meet Mishbee. I must remember to take my journal. Why does this hurt so much? Why am I so hot? It feels as if I'm on fire. I'm so tired, so tired …*

Finally, John fell into a fitful sleep. As soon as she saw that he was finally resting, Elizabeth went about her chores. Later that evening she came in to check on John and found him awake. "Here's some cod liver oil," she told him, holding out a spoon. "Take it."

Joseph stepped into the room behind her. "You'll be all right, boy. Just take the medicine." His words were more confident than his thoughts. He had seen consumption's handiwork many times before, often without happy endings. Joseph remembered hammering the nails into a pine box the past winter for the little girl down the path. He had worked throughout the night preparing the coffin. She was no more than four years old when consumption overcame her. It didn't seem right to build such a tiny coffin for such a young girl, but that was life in this land. Joseph shuddered at the thought of having to make another box for John.

Wearily, John accepted the nasty-tasting cod liver

oil from Elizabeth. He was too weak to rave anymore, and he followed orders meekly. The next day he was supposed to meet Mishbee, but there would be no decorations of red ochre in his immediate future, only the red of his own blood.

CHAPTER 12

"**I**'m not sure he's going to make it," John heard Joseph say in the front room.

Who is Joseph talking about? Who is he talking to? What day is this?

"You shouldn't talk so loud," a voice scolded. "What if he hears you?"

"I wish that were true," Joseph said, lowering his tone, "but I'm afraid he hasn't been able to make much sense of any of us. The poor boy keeps asking for his father's watch. We put it in his hands, but he never remembers that he's got it. It's a shame. Sometimes he recognizes me and sometimes he doesn't."

"Has anyone written his father to tell him of the situation?" the voice asked.

"We've been holding off, hoping John will pull through," Joseph said. "His family has had so much tragedy in the past few years. We wanted to spare his father any unnecessary worry."

"Yes, yes, of course," the voice said.

"He's in pretty rough shape," Joseph said. "He's been coughing a lot and has lost a fair amount of blood. We've been doing our best to keep him alive, but I don't know.

I just don't know. It's been a bad year. Prayers are all we have left."

Then John heard a little girl's voice. He tried to identify it but couldn't quite manage it. "If anyone can get better, John will."

John? Why are they saying my name? What do they mean that prayers are all they have left? What's going on? They're talking about me! I'm the one who's ill, the one they don't think will live. These voices are speaking about my survival!

"Yes, Annie," Joseph said, you're right. If anyone can pull through, it's John. So don't worry."

Annie …? Now it all makes sense. I remember. I'm sick with consumption. It's been going on for days, maybe weeks. The pain, the heat, the blood, the coughing. My mind is a blur and the days have all melted together. I'm so tired of being sick, tired of coughing, tired of blood, tired of lying in this bed …

"If he takes a turn for the better, let me know. I'd like to see him."

John recognized Miss Wells's voice.

"Certainly," Joseph said. "We'll keep you informed. And, of course, we'll be sure to call for you if he improves."

John heard the front door close as someone, obviously Miss Wells, left. A few moments later Joseph walked into his bedroom, parted the curtains, and asked, not really expecting an answer, "John, how are you today?"

"Joseph," John whispered, "please tell me this terrible affliction is over with!"

Joseph's face split into a grin. "Ah, lad, it's good to hear your voice. You look a great deal better today, boy. I won't lie to you. It's been touch and go these many days. You're very fortunate to be talking this morning. Very fortunate indeed. You've had Mrs. Manuel running off her feet tending to you. She's obviously a good nurse, though."

John smiled weakly. "If nothing else, at least I know where I am today. I guess that's a start."

"Yes, that's certainly a good sign."

"How long have I been in bed? It feels like forever."

"It's been several weeks now. But I must say, you really are looking much better this morning."

Weeks in bed! Had Joseph finished the last touches on the schooner himself? And what about Mishbee? John felt a wave of panic! He had worked so hard to communicate with twigs and gestures and now he had missed his meeting with Mishbee. Had she come to the pond weeks ago only to discover his failure to show up?

John had to do something. He couldn't afford to lie in bed one second longer. He had to find Mishbee again.

"Well, then, I have to get up now," he announced to Joseph. "I have to go on a trip. Where's my watch?" He fumbled around, searching for his precious timepiece.

Joseph shook his head. "It's right here beside the bed. You've been asking for it all during your illness." He laughed. "I don't think you'll be going on any trips today. In fact, you won't be going anywhere for at least a couple of more weeks. You're lucky to be alive, and if you want to stay that way, you have to rest. No trips for you just now, my boy."

At that moment Elizabeth strode into the room. "Trips? My goodness, John. You and your trips. When will you ever learn?"

Surrendering weakly to this wise advice, John lay back in bed. It was true. He was in no shape to travel. He had missed Mishbee already, and whether he showed up today or two weeks from now, she probably wouldn't be there, anyway.

John managed to sit up for a few minutes that day and was able to eat a little. For the most part, though, he stared out the window at the ocean for long periods of time, which was all he had the strength to do. Each day, however, he became a little stronger. He began walking around the house somewhat and helped with chores as much as possible. Eventually, he started to feel guilty about not spending time at the shipyard, even though he knew Joseph could easily survive a few weeks without his help.

Several days later he heard a familiar voice. "John, John, look what I brought you." Young Annie came bounding in with a fistful of flowers to put on the table beside John's bed.

"Well, look who's here," John said, pleased.

"It's me."

"A ray of sunshine," John said, smiling.

Annie laughed at his comment. "See these flowers, John? They're everlasting daisies. And these plants here, they're called boy's love. I love the smell of boy's love." She stuck her face in the middle of the fragrant plants and inhaled deeply. The fresh, woody aroma filled the room.

"So they are, Annie. What have you been up to these past few weeks? Have you been a help at home?"

"Of course! I'm always a help. I've been working in the garden with my sister, and I'm still busy picking raspberries. Here, I brought you some. My father says that berries always help keep your strength up."

"Why, thank you very much. Just put them with the flowers."

Annie dumped a heap of runny raspberries on the table. John looked at the unappetizing pile and figured he would dispose of them when she left.

"You scared me, John. I overheard my father and one of his friends talking about you one night. They said you were as good as dead. But they were wrong, weren't they?"

"Yes, Annie. Luckily for me, they were wrong."

She grinned impishly. "Do you think you could take me out in your boat when you get better?"

"Maybe in a while. We'll have to see about that, missy."

Their conversation was interrupted by another familiar voice. "Why, John, you're looking good this morning," Allen said heartily as he entered the bedroom. "It's so good to see you talking again." Allen shifted his weight from one foot to the other, then cleared his throat. "I must say, you certainly keep giving me the frights, this consumption business being one of them, of course. But I'll never forget that time when I lost you in the bush, either. I thought you'd been killed by one of those savages."

Allen was referring to the time John first met Mishbee. Suddenly, John was angry. How could his friend say this? How dare he? John took as deep a breath as he possibly could without hurting himself and bit his tongue. Allen had lost a brother to the Red Indians. He just didn't know any better. But even with that knowledge, John's anger wouldn't go away. Mishbee wasn't a savage. She was a person — a living, breathing person. Emotion welled up uncontrollably within his weak body.

"Allen," John began tactfully, "I'm still very tired. Do you mind letting me get some rest now?"

"That's the proper thing. You do that. Come on there, little Miss Annie. We'll come back another day. Get yourself better now, John."

It was good to see Annie and Allen, but John was relieved that he didn't have to listen to Allen anymore. Seeing that he wouldn't be building any schooners today or travelling to look for Mishbee, John decided to write a letter to his sister:

To my dearest sister,

I hope all is well with you. I deeply regret that I couldn't attend your wedding but know you were a radiant bride, one a brother would be especially proud of. I'm relieved that you found someone as wonderful as George. He's a good man, and I know he'll be good to my big sister. Please give him my best.

I miss you, Ruth. Much has happened to me in the past few weeks, and I don't know where to begin. I must say that I'm pleased to be alive. Unfortunately, I became plagued with consumption. If it hadn't been for the dear attentions of Mrs. Manuel, I probably wouldn't have survived the ordeal. So many people have fallen victim to this dreadful disease on this island. It is so hard to keep death's hand from your door.

It looks as though I'm on the mend now. Bed rest is still required in order for my lungs to heal fully. I'll miss being at the shipyard working on the schooners. But there will be time enough for that in the near future.

I've met many interesting people in this new land. Some I've told you about and others I choose to keep secret. But there is one thing I've learned. There is misunderstanding and intolerance in both the New and the Old Worlds. This infirmity knows no boundary, and I feel the effects of it even here.

I truly hope to come home to visit next year. The sights and sounds of England elude me, and that causes me sadness. Give my regards to Father.

Affectionately,
John

John read over his letter one more time, folded it, then sealed it in an envelope. Soon this correspondence would cross the vast ocean and be read by his loving sister, a thought that cheered him up greatly.

CHAPTER 13

"Time for breakfast, John!" Elizabeth called out.

It was another morning. Quickly, John got out of bed, washed up, then went into the kitchen for some needed nourishment. It felt so good to be up and around again. He was starting to feel like his old self once more. It would be good to walk around without the threat of consumption burning his lungs. His strength was returning, and he was eager to go back and look for Mishbee. He knew he had missed his appointment with her by several weeks, but deep down he hoped she would keep looking for his return. He must try to find her.

"Are you feeling up to coming to the shipyard today, John?" Joseph asked as he finished his tea.

"Yes, I'd like that."

As they left the house and walked slowly towards the shipyard, John thought longingly about getting back to the main island as swiftly as possible to look for Mishbee. When they entered the yard, John couldn't help but admire the schooner he had worked on.

"All finished now," Joseph announced. "Except for a name, of course."

The next day John managed to make his way back to the now-familiar pond. He threw stones in the water, hoping Mishbee would arrive. But after several hours he gave up. Disappointed, he returned to Exploits Island.

John wasn't about to give up so quickly, though. The following day he woke up early and grabbed his journal, determined to revisit the pond on the main island.

"John, you've got to take it easier and space out these trips of yours," Joseph insisted when John strolled into the kitchen fully dressed and intent on another journey.

"Don't worry, Joseph. I'm fine." He couldn't afford to rest. He had to find Mishbee again. Time was running out!

When he arrived at the pond, he sat quietly on the rock. It was a warm day and he soon began to feel tired. Before he knew it he was napping on the ground beside the rock. When he finally opened his eyes, he was staring right at Mishbee. How long had she been there watching him sleep? "Hello," he croaked.

"Hello," she replied, remembering the English greeting.

He studied her for a moment. She looked different, somewhat thinner, her cheeks hollow. Like him, Mishbee appeared tired and worn out as if she had been sick. "I'm sorry I didn't come back when I said I would," he told her. "I was very ill and couldn't."

John started to take his journal out of his bag. He was about to ask Mishbee more words in her language but was halted. She took his arm and pulled him forward, indicating that he was to follow her.

"Just a minute," he said, putting down his journal.

They walked silently past places he had never been before. It was completely unfamiliar territory to him and he began to worry. "Where are you taking me?"

There was no response. Finally, they arrived at a small cave next to a narrow passage of water. Mishbee led him inside.

As John entered the cave, it took a moment for his eyes to adjust to the dimness. Then he was overtaken with indescribable emotion. In front of him he saw moccasins, leggings, a beautiful bone comb, several pendants, and some birchbark baskets. They were all sprinkled with red ochre dust. Why were all these things here? he wondered.

"*No-o-o-o!*" he suddenly cried when the realization hit him. Before him, curled up in a fetal position, lay a body wrapped in birchbark. He recognized the coloured beads in the body's hair. It was the girl who had pulled Mishbee out of the way of Allen's line of fire. The last time he had seen her she was so healthy and so alive. All he could see in his mind was her piercing glare.

This can't be happening, he thought. *It's just a bad dream.*

Suddenly, John was angry. Who had done this to her? Was it Allen? Who had been so cruel to take the precious life from Mishbee's saviour? Had she been shot by a ruthless settler?

He knelt beside the dead girl's body and stared in horror at her face. There, before his very eyes, was the answer to his question. On her face was a trickle of dried blood that had run out from her mouth to her chin. While he had been busy fighting his own battle against consumption, that very disease had taken the life of this young woman.

"I killed her," he moaned. "I killed her."

Mishbee may not have recognized his words, but he

knew she understood all too well his grief. He could see her own immeasurable sorrow in her dark eyes.

"Oobata," Mishbee almost gasped.

"I'm not sure what you mean," John said, trying to understand.

Mishbee pointed at the dead girl. "Oobata." Then she indicated herself. "Mishbee." Next she crossed her fingers. "Oobata, Mishbee."

"Her name's Oobata," John said, nodding. "And she's your sister like I thought."

This news only made John more miserable. He pushed past Mishbee and went out into the fresh air. "I didn't mean to hurt her!" he declared to the elements as if seeking forgiveness there.

He didn't know how long he wept or how much time had passed when he noticed a familiar hand on his arm. Taking a deep breath, he turned around to see Mishbee. Gently, she took his hand to lead him back into the cave.

"Please don't take me back in there!" he protested but followed her nevertheless.

For a long time they sat in silence. Then something strange happened. Mishbee began singing. He had never heard anything like it before. It was as if she were somehow comforting her sister. When she finished her song, she took the pendant that John had repaired so long ago and placed it beside Oobata. She then picked up a small, sharp stone, cut a lock of hair from her own head, and handed it to him.

"For me?" he asked. *"Drona,"* he murmured, remembering the word for hair. "How can I take this from you after all that's happened?" He tried to hand the keepsake back to Mishbee, but she waved him away.

John clutched the lock tightly. "Thank you." Then, taking one last look at Oobata's lifeless body, he said, "I'm so sorry this has happened, Mishbee. I know she was precious to you. A sister always is."

Numbed and dazed by this whole experience, John followed Mishbee back to the pond. He didn't pick up twigs, hoping to arrange another meeting. Instead, he said goodbye to Mishbee, part of him knowing he might never see her again, hoping fervently that she would be safe and find happiness once more despite her current grief.

When John finally arrived at the Manuels' house later that day, he had no recollection of his journey back. The trip and the experience of seeing Mishbee's dead sister had severely sapped his energy. So when he was greeted by Elizabeth at the door, he didn't answer immediately, which alarmed her.

"Are you all right, John? You look pale. I knew another trip would take too much out of you."

"I'm … I'm fine, Mrs. Manuel," John stammered, then went directly to bed.

Sometime later, when Elizabeth called him for supper, he told her he was too tired to eat.

"Well, I never heard such a thing! When you're tired, that's when you really need to eat. You've got to keep your strength up or you'll get sick again."

"No, thank you," John answered in such a firm tone that even Elizabeth knew it was no use to continue the conversation.

The next day John accompanied Joseph to the shipyard. "It's time we name this boat, John," Joseph said as they approached the new schooner. "What will it be?"

John's heart raced a little faster. "Mishbee. I'd like to call it Mishbee."

"That's a curious name, John. What does it mean and how do you spell it?"

"It's someone I once knew who was dear to me," he said, then spelled the name as well as he could for his mentor.

After putting a few hours in at the shipyard, John went home early, telling Joseph he was feeling a bit under the weather. For the rest of that day he lay in bed and stared at the ceiling. Elizabeth came into his room a number of times. She couldn't understand his listlessness. At first she attributed it to a slow recovery from the consumption. "What's wrong, boy?" she kept asking him. But each time John's only reply was a sigh.

The next day John tried to work on the new schooner Joseph and his men were building, but his heart wasn't in it. He was distracted and his work was sloppy, something uncharacteristic for him.

"Maybe you need more rest, John," Joseph suggested at the end of the day. "You had quite a fight with that consumption. Maybe more rest is in order."

John stayed in bed the next two days, but the rest didn't make him any more eager to return to work with Joseph. Something was eating away at him.

That night Joseph went into John's room, hoping to lift his spirits with his news. "I've finally named the schooner, John. Her name's been painted on and it looks quite smart. I decided to use young Annie's name, too, since she's always adding some cheer at the shipyard. So it's official. The new schooner is the *Mishbee Ann*."

John sighed. "It's named then."

After excusing himself, John went for a walk. He needed to get out of the house for a while. On his ramble he met Annie, skipping along as usual.

"Hello, John," she said, overflowing with enthusiasm.

"Hello there, missy," John greeted.

"See what I picked?" she said, showing him her bouquet. "They're for you, John. They're everlasting daisies."

John suddenly became very angry. He grabbed the flowers from the little girl's hand and threw them to the ground. "They aren't everlasting daisies," he snapped. They're dead man's flowers!"

Shocked, Annie began to wail. Then, obviously frightened, she turned and ran towards her home.

Realizing what he had done, John called out, "Annie, I'm sorry! I don't know what came over me."

But Annie kept on running.

Now what have I done? John thought. *I've scared the daylights out of that precious girl.*

John decided to walk to Annie's home. He had to make things right with his little friend. When he reached Annie's house and knocked on the door, the little girl's older sister, Sarah, answered, welcoming him with a scowl. "Annie's mad at you. You made her cry."

"I … I guess I did. I didn't mean to. Could I have a word with her?"

"I don't think she wants to speak to you," Sarah said.

"Please ask her."

Sarah thought for a moment, then said, "Just a minute. Stay here." She retreated inside the house while he waited on the front porch.

A moment later a tear-stained Annie shuffled to the front door, sniffing loudly. "Why did you scream at me, John? I thought you were my friend."

"I am, Annie, and I'm dreadfully sorry for what I did. I've been feeling awful lately, and I took it out on you. I was angry about something else. Really, it had nothing to do with you."

She wasn't going to let John off easily. "You were mean!"

"Yes, very mean."

"You better not be so mean again!"

"I promise I never will."

"Are you sure?"

"Absolutely."

"Then I forgive you."

"Thank you."

"If you weren't angry with me, John, who were you angry with?"

John thought for a moment. "Myself."

"How can someone be angry with himself?"

"Believe me, it can happen. Annie, do you still want that boat ride you asked for when I was sick?"

"Oh, yes, yes!" she squealed with delight.

"Well, ask your mother if you can go tomorrow. We'll go for a ride, but it will be for the entire day."

"The entire day!" she echoed, jumping up and down with excitement.

John went to bed early that night. There was a lot to do tomorrow and he needed the rest. Carefully, he placed the silky black lock of hair Mishbee had given him between the pages of his journal, then blew his candle out.

The next morning John announced to the Manuels, "I'm leaving Exploits Island. I wish to go back to my family. You've done so much for me, Joseph, and taught me so much, but I really need to go back."

"But, John, you're doing such fine work here," Joseph said. "You show so much promise. Maybe you're homesick and need a visit. In fact, a visit would do you a lot of good."

"No, I feel my time here on this island needs to end."

"But why, John?" Elizabeth asked.

He wanted to answer truthfully and tell the Manuels about Mishbee and her people who he felt would never be able to mingle amicably with the settlers because of misunderstandings and disease. He wished to share his remorse and guilt about Oobata who lay in a quiet burial cave, but he couldn't.

"I really need to be with my own family right now," he said simply.

Joseph continued to protest, but nothing his mentor said could sway John. His mind was made up. A ship bound for England was leaving the day after tomorrow and he would be on it.

"I'm going on one more trip to the main island before my departure for England," he informed Elizabeth and Joseph as he headed out the door. Walking briskly, he was soon at Annie's house where he found the little girl waiting for him on the porch.

"Where are we going?" she asked excitedly.

"To a pond" was all he said.

Annie chattered throughout the entire voyage, and John was relieved that he didn't have to make an effort to talk. As soon as he safely secured their boat on the shoreline of the main island, he led Annie to the pond where he had met Mishbee so many times before. This would be his last visit here. For a while he watched Annie scamper and play around the pond, but soon she became restless.

"Let's go for a walk," John suggested, set on fulfilling his real reason for the boat ride.

"Oh, let's!" Annie cried, following him closely.

John had to think hard to retrace the steps he had taken with Mishbee, but eventually he made his way back to the burial cave. He wondered if Mishbee was somewhere in the woods observing him. She could be so quiet that he would never know.

When he and Annie were fairly close to the burial cave, John said, "You stay here for a few minutes, Annie. I have a little errand to do." He noticed a berry bush close by. "Pick some of those berries for the boat ride."

"Why can't I come with you?" she asked.

"I'll just be a few minutes. This is something I must do alone. Be a good girl, all right? And sing a song while I'm gone so I can hear that you're safe."

Annie wasn't pleased with this arrangement, but she reluctantly agreed to do as he asked.

John picked a few everlasting daisies, then made his way to the cave. He felt slightly uncomfortable in the darkness with the dead girl and her belongings. Slowly, he put down the flowers.

"I hope these grow where you've gone to, Oobata. We call them everlasting daisies, like the everlasting memory your people have left with me. Thank you for looking after Mishbee. You certainly saved her life the day Allen almost shot her. I hope your spirit continues to watch out for her in a way I can't. I don't know if I'll be back."

Without hesitation he reached into his pocket and stroked his father's gold watch. Gently, and with determination, he took out the timepiece and placed it alongside the body. "This is where it belongs," he said, certain Mishbee would know it was his and realize he had been here one last time. Then he left to find Annie … and his future.

Historical Notes

The events of this novel take place in the Bay of Exploits in Newfoundland in approximately the year 1800. Although *A Deadly Distance* is fiction, a number of books were consulted in developing the historical and cultural background (see Selected Reading). Several of the characters and events in this story are real.

The Manuel Family of Exploits Island

Many generations of Manuels were well-known merchants and shipbuilders on Exploits Island. They have been a presence in Newfoundland since the mid-eighteenth century. Incidentally, my great-grandfather, Jacob Manuel, was also a shipbuilder who was born there.

John Peyton, Sr.

John Peyton was a businessman who controlled a great deal of the salmon fishing on the Exploits River. He had a reputation for being very brutal towards the Beothuk people. He had two children, John Jr. and Susan.

John Peyton, Jr.

In the early nineteenth century, John Jr. took over his father's salmon-fishing business and also started a shipyard on Exploits Islands. In 1818 he became the justice of the peace for the northern district of Newfoundland. Unlike his father, John Jr. was more benevolent towards the Beothuks. Shanawdithit, who was renamed Nancy, remained in his household on Exploits Island for five years.

Shanawdithit

Shanawdithit was born around the year 1800. She was captured in 1823 and remained as an assistant with household duties in the Peyton residence for five years. Later she went to St. John's, where she died of tuberculosis on June 6, 1829. Shanawdithit was believed to be the last Beothuk. She was buried in an old graveyard on the south side of St. John's Harbour. In 1903 the graveyard was dismantled to make way for a railway.

Mishbee, Oobata, John Harper, Allen, Their Families, and the *Mishbee Ann*

They are not historical. However, they are quite real in the author's imagination!

GLOSSARY

Aichmudyim: Beothuk word for devil.

Beothuks: An extinct First Nations people of the island of Newfoundland who were Algonquian-speaking
hunter-gatherers. They may have been the aboriginal people referred to as *skraelings* in the Vikings' sa-
gas, and if so, were first encountered by Europeans
around the early eleventh century. After the voyage to
Newfoundland in 1497 of the Italian John Cabot, who
was in the employ of the English, European contact with
the Beothuks increased greatly as the white man's fishing stations, fur trapping, and then settlements spread
throughout the island. Early European settlers and trappers called the Beothuks "Red Indians" because of the
red ochre the aboriginal people covered their bodies
with. Eventually, this term was applied to First Nations
people in general, even those to whom red ochre had no
cultural significance whatsoever. The Beothuks probably
never numbered much more than a couple of thousand
people, but by the late eighteenth century their popula-
tion had dwindled to likely a few hundred at best. The
reduction in numbers was probably due to a number of
factors, including lack of resistance to European diseases
such as tuberculosis, increasingly fierce competition with

Europeans for traditional sources of food such as fish and game, and ever more violent encounters with European settlers. The woman Shanawdithit, who died in 1829 of tuberculosis, is said to have been the last Beothuk, though some say a few Beothuks may have survived and intermarried with other First Nations people.

Birchbark: The bark of the paper birch tree is a strong and water-resistant cardboard-like substance that can be easily cut, bent, and sewn. To First Nations people, voyageurs, and early European settlers, it was valuable as a building, crafting, and writing material. Today birchbark remains popular for various handicrafts and arts. Birchbark also contains substances of medicinal and chemical interest.

Consumption: See **Tuberculosis**.

Cormorant: A medium to large coastal seabird commonly found throughout most of the world.

Drona: Beothuk word for hair.

Ebanthoo: Beothuk word for water.

Great Auk: A flightless, web-footed, extinct black-and-white bird that was once found in great numbers on islands off Canada's East Coast and in Greenland, Iceland, Norway, Ireland, and Great Britain. The bird became extinct by the middle of the nineteenth century.

Kittiwake: A type of gull widely dispersed in North America and Europe, the kittiwake's name is derived from its distinctive call.

Mamateek: Beothuk word for dwelling.

Moosin: Beothuk word for moccasin or shoe.

Murre: Largely found in North America and Europe, this seabird congregates and breeds in noisy colonies on islands, rocky shores, cliffs, and sea stacks.

Odeman: Beothuk word for red ochre.

Osweet: Beothuk word for caribou.

Paushee: Beothuk word for birchbark.

Red Ochre: A pigment extracted from iron oxide clay deposits in Newfoundland, red ochre was a substance that held great significance in the culture of the Beothuks, who used it to coat their implements, their bodies, and the remains of their dead. The colour red played an important role in Beothuk tribal identity. Forcing disgraced band members to remove the pigment was viewed as a very serious punishment. It is quite likely that the red hue also had spiritual overtones for Beothuks. The extensive use of red ochre caused Europeans to name the Beothuks "Red Indians."

Schooner: A ship with two or more masts, the foremast being smaller than the other masts.

Tabus: Beothuk word for rules or rituals.

Tilt: A term in Newfoundland that refers to a temporary shelter such as a cabin or shack.

Tuberculosis: A highly infectious bacterial disease, often called consumption in previous times, tuberculosis is characterized by tubercles (small, rounded swellings or lesions) in the body's organs, especially the lungs. Once a disease that plagued much of the world, including North America, tuberculosis is still a major problem in many developing countries and has seen a resurgence even in places where it had almost been eradicated, though antibiotics and vaccines are now available to combat it. However, new, drug-resistant strains of the disease continue to manifest themselves. It is estimated today that more than fifteen million people in the world have active tuberculosis and that approximately two million people die of the disease each year.

Winterhousing: The tradition in Newfoundland of moving to sheltered homesteads in winter.

Selected Reading

Evans, Calvin. *For Love of a Woman*. St. John's, NF: Harry Cuff Publications Ltd., 1992.

Harris, Michael. *Rare Ambition*. Toronto: Penguin Books, 1992.

Howley, James P. *The Beothuks or Red Indians: The Aboriginal Inhabitants of Newfoundland*. London: Cambridge University Press, 1915.

Lacy, Reverend Garland. *The Manuels of Exploits, Newfoundland*. Privately Printed, 1970.

Marshall, Ingeborg. *A History and Ethnography of the Beothuk*. Montreal: McGill-Queen's University Press, 1966.

_____. *Reports and Letters by George Christopher Pulling Relating to the Beothuk Indians of Newfoundland*. St. John's, NF: Breakwater Books, 1989.

_____. *The Beothuk of Newfoundland: A Vanished People*. St. John's, NF: Breakwater Books, 1989.

Rowe, Frederick W. *Extinction: The Beothuks of Newfoundland*. Toronto: McGraw-Hill Ryerson, 1977.